"Look at the tree, Tim," Beth murmured encouragingly, conscious of James's silent approach across the carpet

Obligingly Timmy focused his eyes briefly in the direction she'd requested and then, evidently deciding she'd been sufficiently humored, returned to his ceiling inspection.

"Blasé at six months?" James lifted a dark eyebrow as he stretched up a lean hand and switched on the wall lights.

At the sound of his uncle's voice, Timmy immediately turned his head, and with a delighted smile began flapping his arms toward him.

"I'll take him, shall I?" James drawled.

Not deceived for a second by the airy nonchalance in his voice, Beth placed Timmy in the strong, waiting arms, flicking a glance upward into the dark face. Unobserved, her eyes moved over the square _____ ____ ___ ____ ___ _ the decisive m_____ he ever going to b_____ without remem_____

D0968008

Dear Reader,

A special delivery! We are proud to announce the latest arrival in our yearlong bouncing baby series! This series is all about the true labor of love—parenthood and how to survive it! Because, as our heroes and heroines are about to discover, two's company and three (or four, or five) is a family!

This month it's the turn of Rosemary Gibson with *Baby in the Boardroom*. Next month's arrival will be (#3484) *Reform of the Rake* by Catherine George.

Happy reading!

The Editors

BABY BOOM

Because two's company and three
(or four...or five) is a family!

Baby in the Boardroom
Rosemary Gibson

Harlequin Books

TORONTO • NEW YORK • LONDON
AMSTERDAM • PARIS • SYDNEY • HAMBURG
STOCKHOLM • ATHENS • TOKYO • MILAN
MADRID • WARSAW • BUDAPEST • AUCKLAND

ISBN 0-373-03481-4

BABY IN THE BOARDROOM

First North American Publication 1997.

CHAPTER ONE

'I *NEED* you, Beth.'

It took several seconds for the deep voice at the other end of the telephone to penetrate into Beth Sinclair's sleep-befuddled brain.

'What?' she mumbled, throwing back the duvet cover and swinging her legs out of the bed. She glanced blearily at the alarm clock on her bedside table and yelped in disbelief. 'James Fenner, do you know what time it is?' she demanded. 'Half past two in the morning...'

'I'm well aware of the time,' he answered tersely. 'But it's urgent.'

'Urgent?' she muttered incredulously, sweeping a lock of silky brown hair over her shoulder with her free hand. 'I don't care how urgent it is, it'll have to wait until morning.' She'd never supposed that working as PA for the workaholic chairman of Stanton Enterprises was going to be easy, had accepted that it wouldn't be a nine-to-five job, but this was bordering on lunacy.

'I've done my ten-hour stint today and nothing in the world is going to drag me back to the office at this ungodly hour of the—'

'I'm not at the office,' he cut through with barely veiled impatience. 'I'm at my flat...'

'I don't care where you are...'

'And it's a personal matter.'

'Personal?' Beth echoed sceptically. Was this just an intriguing carrot with which to snare her? A carrot that would miraculously turn into a pile of papers and a computer screen when she arrived at his flat? It was impossible to imagine her self-sufficient, coolly competent employer with any type of personal problem that he couldn't deal with himself. Or with the assistance of one of those carbon-copy blondes with six-foot-long legs who wafted into the office to whisk him off for long lunches. Presumably he could differentiate between the lookalikes, but she'd certainly had difficulty at times. The only distinguishing feature about Julia Summers—the current woman in his life—was that she seemed to have lasted rather longer than her predecessors.

'The taxi will be there in about ten minutes,' the deep voice growled in her ear. 'And bring an overnight case.'

Beth surveyed the receiver in her hand with thoughtful, thick-lashed hazel eyes. 'I haven't said I'll come yet,' she said serenely. 'I'll have to think it over.'

'Think it over in the goddamn taxi!'

There was a short, abrupt silence as if, Beth decided, the dark-haired man on the end of the line didn't quite trust himself to continue. After all, he was requesting a favour, and had to monitor his language accordingly. Something, she thought wryly, he didn't always manage to do at the office.

'The taxi will be there in about five minutes now,' he finally grated.

'Arrogant, conceited, selfish swine,' Beth mumbled

under her breath, already reaching out for the volu-
minous cream sweater draped over her bedroom chair.

'What was that?'

'I just said I'll be ready in no time,' she said cheerfully, and raised her eyebrows as, with a muttered,
incoherent grunt, the line went dead.

She must be certifiable, Beth thought incredulously
some twenty minutes later as she sat in the back of
the taxi, her small overnight case balanced on her
jean-clad knees. What on earth was she doing, haring
across London at this hour? She should have discon-
nected the telephone the moment she'd heard James
Fenner's voice. He hadn't even asked her to come;
he'd simply issued an imperious summons, the pre-
ordered taxi indicating that it had never occurred to
him that she wouldn't obey it. She was so weak, she
berated herself mournfully, gazing out into the dark
city streets. Even the Christmas illuminations had
been switched off.

'Here you are.' The taxi driver drew up in front of
the prestigious block of luxury flats.

'Thank you,' Beth murmured, wondering as she
scrambled out whether it was her own sudden self-
consciousness that made her imagine the speculative
look in the driver's eye. She dug her purse out of her
coat pocket.

'It's on Mr Fenner's account.'

Well, that was something, Beth thought grudgingly.
Although she had fully intended submitting an ex-
pense claim for the fare anyway.

'I'll watch until you're safely in,' the taxi driver
said reassuringly, as if misconstruing her slight hesitancy as she glanced up at the imposing building.

She smiled back. It wasn't the deserted streets that she found unnerving, it was the man waiting for her on the third floor, she thought wryly.

He must have been watching out for the taxi because he responded immediately when she pressed the buzzer, releasing the outside door which closed smoothly behind her as she entered the building.

Pausing for a second in the plushly carpeted foyer to get her bearings, she made her way to the lift. In the eighteen months she'd worked for James Fenner she'd only ever been to his flat once, to bring him some papers to sign when he'd had flu. On that occasion, though, she'd not got further than the hall— her entry to the sick bay had been barred by a chic, blonde ministering angel.

Stepping out of the lift, Beth crossed the corridor and stared at the door facing her. She suddenly felt quite ridiculously nervous. Dealing with James Fenner at work was one thing, but seeing him in the informality of his home at this hour of the morning was something altogether different.

She shook herself irritably. She wasn't some teenager with a crush on the boss. She was twenty-three years old, and any romantic notions she might have once harboured about James Fenner had been ruthlessly buried a long time ago.

Taking a deep breath, she knocked briskly on the door.

It swung open almost instantly.

'Do you have to make such a goddamn noise?' James Fenner towered over her. 'And don't slam the door, whatever you do. I think I've finally managed to get him to sleep.'

Great, Beth thought. And it's nice to see you too. Scowling, she followed the retreating figure into the spacious hall. 'Managed to get who to sleep?' she enquired, handing James her coat and small case.

He didn't answer, his narrowed blue eyes sweeping over her tumbled curtain of glossy brown hair and then dropping to the baggy cream sweater and slim-fitting jeans.

'You look different,' he muttered disapprovingly.

Thanks for the ego trip, Beth seethed. 'I look like someone who has been dragged out of their bed at half-two in the morning,' she said bitterly. It was, she realised, the first time James had seen her attired in anything but the severely tailored suits she wore in the office.

'It's your hair...'

OK, she looked a mess, but there was no need to keep pressing the point, Beth thought, aggrieved. She'd barely had time to run a comb through her hair, let alone arrange it in the neat chignon she adopted for work. 'I might tell you you're no oil painting at this hour of the morning either, Mr Fenner.'

Which was a downright lie, she admitted with an uncomfortable dip of her stomach. It was completely unfair, but with his thick, dark hair rumpled, his strong jawline and decisive square chin shadowed by stubble, and dressed in black denims and an open-necked blue shirt, James Fenner simply looked bla-tantly and devastatingly masculine.

'So why exactly have you dragged me halfway across London?' she demanded, tilting her head up-wards, even more aware than usual of his height and the width of his powerful shoulders. 'What on earth

was that?' She spun round as she heard a plaintive
wail.

'Oh, hell!' James Fenner strode down the hall.
'You've gone and woken him up.'

'It's a baby!' Beth scurried after him, her eyes wide
with astonishment. 'What on earth are you doing with
a baby in your flat?'

He paused with his hand on the bedroom door and
looked down into her suspicious, upturned face. 'Before you go jumping to any conclusions,' he said
dryly, 'Timmy is my nephew.'

He pushed open the door, the light from the hall
flooding the bedroom, illuminating the small, tearful
figure sitting forlornly at one end of the travel cot.

'Oh, you poor little poppet.' Instinctively Beth
moved towards the cot and swept the baby up in her
arms.

'It's all so strange, isn't it?' she murmured softly,
her slim body swaying from side to side as she rocked
him soothingly. 'So what's the matter? Are you hungry?'

'Hungry?' James Fenner muttered under his breath.
'I've done nothing but feed, water and change him for
the last two hours.'

Large blue eyes surveyed Beth gravely and then the
small face, surrounded by a halo of golden curls,
creased into a grin. Her heart suddenly squeezing,
Beth grinned back.

'He's adorable.' Gently she ran a caressing finger
over a soft pink cheek. 'How old is he?'

'Adorable?' James grunted. 'You wouldn't have
said that if you'd been here half an hour ago,' he

muttered darkly. 'A couple of months,' he added vaguely.

'A couple of months?' Beth scoffed. Not unless he was some sort of child prodigy! His blue eyes hazing over, Timmy began sucking furiously on his thumb. 'Surely you know how old he is?' She gave a quick, disbelieving glance at the figure filling the open doorway.

'He was born on my birthday…'

'June the eighteenth,' Beth said without thinking, and then flushed as she saw the flicker of surprise on the dark face. Oh, damn, she cursed silently. 'That makes him six months,' she calculated quickly. Exactly thirty-five years his uncle's junior.

She looked down into the small face and saw the golden eyelashes begin to flicker down. Humming softly under her breath, she laid the sleeping infant carefully down in his cot. She pulled up the cover and very gently extracted his tiny thumb from his mouth. He stirred slightly and then lay still. More than a little surprised by her success, Beth tiptoed silently from the room.

'Beginner's luck,' James informed her, his eyes unreadable. 'Coffee?'

He led her into the spacious, airy lounge, indicating with a wave of his hand that she should take a seat, and disappeared in the direction of the kitchen that Beth had glimpsed earlier.

Muffling a yawn, she sat down on an armchair beside a low table, her gaze wandering curiously around the room. It was grey-carpeted, like the hall, and the walls were cream, adorned by three framed, enlarged photographs of mountains, only one of which she recognised—the Matterhorn. She hazarded a guess that the large cream drapes at the far end of the room concealed French windows leading out onto a balcony.

The subtle decor was undoubtedly restful, the furniture obviously expensive and of a good quality, but the room had a transient feel to it. There was no real impression of the owner's strong personality, no clutter, no collection of mementos or curios.

But then Beth doubted that James Fenner spent much time here except to eat and sleep. On the rare weekends he wasn't in his office, he disappeared down to his cottage in Dorset. Whether he was accompanied on these trips or went alone she had no idea. She and James Fenner, Beth mused wryly, weren't in the habit of exchanging personal confidences over their mid-morning coffee. She glanced up as he walked into the room carrying two mugs.

'White, no sugar.' He placed a mug on the table beside her.

She nodded her thanks. It was ridiculous to feel that swift glow of warmth because he'd remembered something as trivial as the way she drank her coffee.

She took a sip from her mug, and then surveyed him inquiringly over the rim as he folded his long frame into the opposite chair.

'Caroline, my sister, turned up with Timmy about nine o'clock this evening.' He answered her unspoken question. Stretching out his long legs, he folded his arms idly behind his head, the movement causing his shirt to tauten over his powerful shoulders. Beth studied her coffee-mug. 'Mike, her husband, who's been working out in Madagascar, has been taken into hospital with some sort of virus. It's not life-threatening, but he won't be fit enough to travel home for some time.'

'And your sister's gone out to be with him?' Beth raised her eyes to his face, her gaze moving swiftly over the familiar, rugged masculine features.

'She went over to Amsterdam tonight and she'll fly out of Schiphol on a connecting flight first thing in the morning.' He took a sip of coffee. 'Caroline managed to contact an agency before she left, and had arranged for me to interview a temporary nanny to-morrow.'

'So you woke me up in the middle of the night because you couldn't cope with a tiny baby for a few hours?' Beth asked dryly. Why hadn't he called on Julia for assistance? Not that, from the glimpses Beth had had of her in James's office, the cool, long-legged blonde had struck her as the overly maternal type.

'Oh, I could cope with Timmy all right,' James informed her loftily, and then his straight mouth quirked wryly. 'It was just that Timmy couldn't seem to cope with me.' He paused and added casually, 'Caroline and Mike named him after me—James Timothy—although they use his second name...'

Beth hid her smile, not fooled in the least by the casual tone. There was no mistaking the underlying pride and pleasure in his voice. So, contrary to what she'd often thought, James Fenner was capable of normal human emotion occasionally.

Her eyes flicked over the long, lean form. Despite the indolence of his posture he still exuded a latent energy. His eyes, darkened to navy in the dim lighting, were completely alert, showing no sign of fatigue.

Unlike hers, which felt itchy with lack of sleep. Did he never switch off? she wondered. Did he never completely relax?

As if aware of her scrutiny James looked up at her, and Beth quickly focused her attention on one of the three framed photographs on the wall. He turned his head slightly, following her gaze.

'I've climbed all three,' he said unexpectedly.

Startled, Beth's hazel eyes jerked back to his face. 'I didn't know you were a climber.' Although, on reflection, it wasn't altogether surprising that the activity should appeal to this tough, resourceful man. He would relish the physical and mental challenge, competing not against other men but against himself. Raising her eyes, she surveyed each formidable peak in turn and shuddered, recalling the number of climbing tragedies reported by the media each year.

'Past tense,' James murmured regretfully. 'I don't have the time any more.'

'The lure of money and power,' Beth muttered acidly, hiding the relief that washed over her.

He raised a dark eyebrow. 'Is that how you think of me? An avaricious megalomaniac?'

The shutters dropped over Beth's eyes as she heard the teasing note in his voice. She looked at him with contrived indifference. 'I don't think of you as anything,' she said shortly. 'As long as you pay my monthly cheque on time...' She shrugged.

Of course, she didn't think of him in those terms. His authority was unquestionable, but James Fenner was no power-hungry tycoon. It was, Beth was certain, the challenge of operating a successful business that attracted him, the wealth and influence merely by-products of that success.

'You don't approve of me or my lifestyle, do you, Beth?' James's mouth quirked.

'I just wouldn't want to emulate it,' she retorted. 'There's more to life than—' She shut her mouth quickly.

'Than what?' he prompted.

OK, you've asked for it, James Fenner. 'Than a succession of transient, casual relationships.' Beth threw her hands wide. 'Than a flat that looks like a hotel suite...' Oh, hell, she thought, aware of the silence as her voice trailed off. Then, to her disbelief, James Fenner threw back his head and laughed, his teeth white and even against his tanned skin.

'You sound,' he drawled, 'just like my sister. In fact,' he mused, his eyes moving over Beth's neat features, 'you are a lot like her.'

Oh, wonderful. Beth studied the grey carpet. That was just what she needed—to remind him of his sister.

'Except Caroline was never particularly career-minded or ambitious.'

Beth blinked. Was that how he saw her—ambitious and career-minded? She enjoyed the mental stimulus of working for James, prided herself on her competence. But she had no desire to step any higher on the corporate ladder, had no executive ambition. Of course, she might have made those claims at her interview, she remembered with a jolt...

'So what am I missing out on?' James raised a quizzical dark eyebrow.

Total commitment to another human being and not

just a balance sheet. A home. A family. Beth could just imagine the snort of derision he would give if she voiced the words out loud. If James Fenner had any desire to change his bachelor existence, he would doubtless have already done so.

Abruptly she rose to her feet, leaving his question unanswered.

'You might be able to survive on three hours' sleep a night, but I can't,' she said curtly, wondering why she suddenly felt so angry with him. Because she was tired? Because he was as insensitive as a brick wall? Because of all those long-legged blondes who didn't remind him of his sister...?

'I'll show you to your room.' James got up in a swift, controlled movement, following her out of the lounge. Retrieving her small overnight case, he guided her down the hall, pausing outside Timmy's room to look in through the half-open door.

Timmy was fast asleep, lying in a crouched position, his tiny little haunches in the air. Automatically Beth glanced up at James, and saw the reflection of her own amusement on his face as he gazed down at his namesake. As her eyes moved swiftly over the strong, assured face and then dropped back to the small, vulnerable infant, her stomach muscles clenched in a fierce knot, an incomprehensible yearning sweeping over her with an intensity that was almost a physical pain.

Shaken, she followed James on down the hall, keeping her face deliberately averted from the all too discerning blue eyes.

He threw open a door at the end of the hall and flicked on the light. The room beyond was as luxuriously decorated and furnished as the rest of the flat, and had the same air of emptiness.

Standing aside to allow Beth through, James remained on the threshold. 'You'll find everything you need—towels, soap—in there.' He indicated the *en suite* bathroom visible through the open door at the far end of the bedroom.

'Thank you,' Beth muttered as he handed her the small case. She felt absurdly awkward, as gauche as a teenager, uneasily conscious of the sudden silence. She forced herself to look up at him. He was frowning, his eyes moving slowly over her face, as if inspecting each individual feature in turn—her wide-spaced hazel eyes, high cheekbones, neat, straight nose. His gaze dropped to the curve of her mouth...

Beth couldn't move; her throat constricting. She could see her reflection in the dark blue eyes...

'Goodnight, Beth.' His voice muffled, James abruptly spun round and strode down the hall.

Closing the door, Beth leant back against it, waiting until she regained control of her erratic breathing. Oh, come on, you didn't seriously think he was going to kiss you? she berated herself. Her mouth curved mockingly as she glimpsed her reflection in the full-length mirror on the door of the fitted wardrobe. Her hair was dishevelled, her eyes gritty and dark-shadowed from weariness.

She grinned wryly, muffling a yawn. James Fenner had never evinced the slightest personal interest in her, and she somehow doubted that her less than *soignée* appearance tonight had suddenly sparked off some dormant passion!

Heaving a resigned sigh, she fished out the baggy T-shirt she wore in bed and headed for the bathroom.

Beth's eyes flickered open and she frowned, momentarily disorientated as she gazed up at the unfamiliar white ceiling. Recollection returned, and with it awareness of the rays of sunshine filtering through the green curtains. What time was it...? She reached for her wristwatch on the bedside table and groaned in disbelief. Ten o'clock. Oh, good grief—Timmy.

Scrambling out of bed, she tugged her jeans and sweater over her T-shirt, darted across the room and flung the door open. But there was no accusatory roar of a small, hungry voice.

Raking her fingers through her hair, she padded swiftly down the hall. Timmy's bedroom door was open, the cot vacant. Automatically she began to head for the kitchen and paused, flicking a glance through the half-open lounge door as she heard the murmur of voices.

Timmy, looking angelic in a blue romper suit, his hair a mass of golden curls, was sitting contentedly on the lap of a pleasant-faced, capable-looking middle-aged woman. James was hidden from Beth's view, but she could hear the deep rumble of his voice.

Beth grinned as she crept past quietly, wondering sympathetically if the prospective nanny was undergoing the same tough ordeal that she had experienced at her interview.

As she entered the modern kitchen, her eyes immediately registered the bright red plastic bowl and the bottle which, together with a plate and mug, were stacked neatly by the dishwasher. Why hadn't James woken her this morning? Out of consideration?

She snorted dismissively. No. Simply because, despite his profession last night, he was obviously perfectly capable of tending to his young nephew without any assistance from her. In fact she couldn't envisage a situation in which James Fenner would ever find himself at a loss. So why had he telephoned her last night? she wondered grumpily. He evidently didn't need her.

'Redundant. Superfluous to all requirements,' Beth muttered grouchily as she touched the side of the coffee-pot on the table. Still hot. Opening wall units at random until she discovered a mug, she filled it with coffee and carried it back to her bedroom, her lips twitching as she caught sight of her disgruntled expression in the mirror. So what had got into her this bright, sunny morning?

After gulping down the coffee, she had a swift shower. Clad once again in her jeans and sweater, she sat at the dressing-table and combed her damp hair, spreading it over her shoulders to dry. Applying a light coat of mascara to her long brown lashes and a discreet lip gloss to her mouth, she stood up, feeling slightly more equipped to deal with the world—and one male inhabitant of it in particular.

Having repacked her small case, she picked it up in one hand, grabbed her dirty mug in the other and, giving the room one last, swift glance, headed out into the hall. The lounge was vacant as she passed it, the interview presumably over.

Depositing her case by the coat stand, still clutching her mug, she pushed open the kitchen door.

His tiny nephew perched on his knees, James was sitting at the table reading out loud from the business section of the newspaper spread out in front of him. Timmy was listening with round, fascinated blue eyes, patting the paper enthusiastically with his small pink hands to mark his evident approval of the subject matter.

A mini tycoon in the making, Beth thought, suppressing her gurgle of laughter as two pairs of blue eyes focused on her.

'Good morning,' she said in her best, cheerful, not-a-care-in-the-world voice as she discarded her mug in the sink. Bracing herself for some caustic comment on her tardiness, she was taken aback when James smiled up at her lazily. Clean-shaven, he was dressed casually in blue jeans and an open-necked dark green shirt, the sleeves of which were folded back on his lean, muscular forearms.

'I'm just going to make some more coffee. Would you like one?'

Giving her no time to reply, obviously taking her assent for granted, his strong arms tightened round his nephew and he rose to his feet.

'Sit down.' He indicated his vacant chair.

Beth hesitated fractionally before doing so, feeling the familiar prickle of resentment and irritation. Why did James Fenner make everything, even trivialities, sound like a command, and always automatically assume that she was only too willing to acquiesce to his every wish?

Then, as he gently deposited Timmy into her arms, she forgot everything and smiled down into the solemn blue eyes.

'Tied up any major deals this morning?' she queried, stroking the silky tail of hair at the nape of
Timmy's neck. Dragging the words of a hitherto-
forgotten nursery rhyme from the recesses of her
childhood memory, she began to sing softly, bouncing
Timmy up and down in time to the rhythm.

He burst into delighted chuckles, flaying his tiny
fists in the air. Hugging him, Beth planted a swift kiss
on the top of his head.

'So when does the nanny start?' she murmured,
glancing up.

James was leaning back against the sink unit, arms
folded across his deep chest as he waited for the kettle
to boil. 'She doesn't,' he said briskly. 'She wasn't
suitable.'

Beth raised her eyebrows.

He shrugged his broad shoulders. 'Timmy didn't
like her,' he said dismissively.

'He told you that?' Beth murmured dryly. From the
brief glimpse she'd had, the nanny had looked eminently suitable, and Timmy had looked perfectly
happy.

'We discussed it at great length and came to a joint
democratic decision,' James assured her airily.

Beth's lips twitched. 'So what are you going to do
now? Hey, that's my hair, you great big bully. Pick
on someone your own size.' As Timmy chuckled un-
repentantly, Beth grinned down at him, and continued
talking to James. 'Arrange some more interviews?'

'I don't think that will really be necessary.'

Frowning, Beth glanced up, her eyes instantly darkening with suspicion as they moved over the carved,
masculine features. James was studying her with the

speculative thoughtfulness she had long ago learned to distrust. It was the same pensiveness with which he regarded her before informing her that he required her to work over a weekend for which she'd already made much looked forward to social arrangements.

His blue eyes locked with hers.

'No,' she said adamantly. 'Don't even think of it! Do I look like Mary Poppins?'

The corners of the straight, firm mouth quirked upwards.

'No,' Beth repeated, glaring at him. One glib smile and he thought she'd be putty in his hands, willing to totally disrupt her life because of him. Well, it wasn't going to work; not this time! Deliberately she dropped her gaze.

Timmy beamed enchantingly up at her.

And you are far too young to start employing those sorts of tactics, Beth reproved him silently. Do you want to grow up like your uncle James?

Her eyes flicked to the dark head and then back to the small, fair one.

'No,' she said weakly for the third and final time. 'Absolutely not...'

CHAPTER TWO

IT MUST have been sheer chance, Beth decided, that Timmy chose that precise moment to look up at his uncle. And she must surely have imagined that conspiratorial, exasperated man-to-man exchange that implied she was simply being capricious.

She was aware of the sudden silence—James's usual tactic whenever she was staging a minor rebellion. He never argued with her, never attempted to persuade her. He simply sat back until she'd run out of steam and waited for her to crack.

'I've never looked after a baby before,' she protested unconvincingly.

'Timmy'll show you the ropes,' James assured her briskly. 'He'll soon let you know if you're not coming up to scratch.'

Like uncle, like nephew? Beth surveyed Timmy thoughtfully as he patted her experimentally on the nose. 'Just you be very careful whom you adopt as a role model, little one,' she warned under her breath, watching James out of the corner of her eye as he rummaged about in a drawer.

'Here.' He handed her a folded sheet of paper.

Beth raised her eyebrows. 'Timmy comes with instructions?' She unfolded the paper, immediately recognising James's distinctive handwriting, and grinned. Presumably following his sister's general guidelines, he'd meticulously drawn up a detailed timetable of Timmy's daily routine.

'There is just one small detail you seem to have overlooked.' Beth flicked James an upward glance, and was disconcerted to discover that he was watching her, his blue, fathomless eyes resting intently on her face. 'You, um, seem to have forgotten that I already have a job.'

He shrugged his broad shoulders dismissively. 'I'll employ a temp to cover for you until Caroline's back. It should only be for a week or so.' With an impatient, lean hand he raked back an errant lock of thick hair that had tumbled wilfully across his forehead.

She was that easy to replace? So much for the illusion that she was fast becoming indispensable at work, Beth thought wryly, her mouth curving as she looked down at Timmy. Exhausted by the strain of interviews and high finance, he had fallen asleep, his golden head nestling against her breast. Gently Beth removed the thumb from his mouth.

'Hmm. He's ahead of schedule. He's not due for his nap yet,' James grunted, leaning across the table to consult the paper in front of Beth.

'What would you like me to do? Wake Timmy up and tell him?' Beth enquired dryly, uncomfortably aware of James's closeness, her sense of smell teased by the subtle fragrance of expensive aftershave. Her eyes were drawn, against her will, to the sprinkle of fine dark hair that trailed up his forearms and disappeared beneath the folded sleeve of his shirt.

'I'll pop him in his cot.' Abruptly she rose to her feet, aware that by doing so she had tacitly accepted her new role.

A role, she realised as she entered Timmy's bed-room, that she was rather looking forward to. Laying Timmy down in his cot, she smiled at him. He was certainly far more restful to be with than his uncle; he had a far more appealing disposition. She was going to enjoy the temporary respite from James Fenner. Except on her arrival each morning and his return from the office at night, she would barely see him.

She hummed as she made her way down the hall. Long, leisurely walks in the park if the weather was good... She grinned. The new temp was welcome to James Fenner. Welcome to his monosyllabic grunts and to the assumption that she was a mind-reader. Welcome to working a twelve-hour day with only a half-eaten sandwich for lunch. Welcome to—

'Beth?'

'Coming,' she sang out sweetly, tracing the impatient voice to the room next to the kitchen. Wasn't Timmy supposed to be the demanding one?

James was sitting behind a paper-strewn desk, talking on the telephone. Looking across at her, he indicated with a wave of his left hand that she should take a seat until he'd finished his call.

She remained standing, her eyes wandering around the room, absorbing the fax machine and computer. She might have guessed that he'd have an office at home. Didn't he ever stop working? Did nothing else matter to him?

A ray of sunshine filtered through the window and glinted on his bowed head. The wayward lock had fallen over his forehead again, and Beth stiffened, shaken by the sudden longing to sweep it back, to twine her fingers through the thick richness of his hair. She couldn't quite meet his eyes as he looked up.

'I've asked Mrs Andrews, the caretaker's wife, to mind Timmy while you go back to your flat.'

'You have?' Beth asked cautiously. Mind-reading time again.

'Presumably you'd like the occasional change of clothes over the next few days?'

Beth jolted, comprehension dawning. 'I'm going to be a residential nanny? Live-in staff?' she asked with a flippancy she was far from feeling. It hadn't occurred to her that he would expect her to move into the flat, though in retrospect it probably should have.

'Timmy doesn't clock off at five every night,' James murmured wryly.

Beth hesitated. 'I just assumed that you'd take over the late shift...' Working for James was one thing; living under his roof twenty-four hours a day, for whatever reason, was something else altogether, she thought uneasily.

'I don't clock off at five either,' he reminded her. He paused. 'It would be far more practical if you stayed here rather than rushing backwards and forwards at all times of the day and night.'

Beth avoided his gaze. 'Far more practical,' she agreed, her expression determinedly impassive.

'I'll order a taxi. And you'll need these.' Pulling open the desk drawer, he extracted a set of keys and held them out to her. 'The larger one fits the outer door.'

Beth nodded, instantly aware of the fleeting, impersonal brush of the lean fingers against hers as he deposited the keys into her outstretched palm.

'I'll fetch my coat.' She started for the door.

'Beth?'

She glanced back over her shoulder as the deep voice halted her.

'Thank you,' he said quietly. The blue eyes drew and held hers for a brief second and then, stretching out a long arm, he picked up the telephone.

'And thanks for giving Timmy his lunch, Mrs Andrews,' Beth murmured gratefully as she ushered the older woman down the hall to the door. The trip to and from her flat had taken her longer than she'd anticipated.

'I've a grandson the same age,' Mrs Andrews smiled. 'My daughter drops by with him most afternoons. Bring Timmy down some time and meet them.'

'Thank you. I will.' Beth smiled back. She'd taken an instant liking to the plump, motherly woman whom she'd discovered James employed as a part-time housekeeper. Closing the door, Beth made her way back to the sitting room, the faint smell of polish indicating that Mrs Andrews had been busy in her absence.

Timmy, temporarily ensconced in his play-pen, waved a white rabbit at her as she walked in.

'Fancy helping me unpack?' Beth enquired, scooping him up in her arms and carrying him into the hall and down to her bedroom. She sat him in the middle of the carpet and, lifting her suitcase onto the bed, began to remove the contents and place them in the wardrobe.

'Mostly jeans and jumpers,' she explained to her

fascinated small audience, and then tugged out a black silk jersey-dress. 'Why I brought this I don't know,' she mused. 'What do you think?' She held it up to her slim figure.

Timmy chuckled.

'Smoothie.'

Beth hung up the dress in the wardrobe and then, with a feeling of complete unreality, surveyed the green and cream room. What was she doing here in James's home? she wondered in disbelief. How had she ever allowed herself to be manipulated into this situation?

'You're not the problem,' she assured Timmy swiftly with a sigh. Picking him up in her arms, she held him up to the wardrobe mirror. Round-eyed, he patted his reflection admiringly. 'It's your uncle.'

Moving over to the bed, she sat down with Timmy on her lap. 'You're not going to believe this, but when I first met your uncle James I was a bit bowled over. I suppose I'd just never met anyone like him before.' Men like James Fenner simply hadn't existed in the small rural community in which she'd been brought up by a maiden aunt.

'Of course, I'm over that silly crush, infatuation— whatever—now,' she said hastily, but the conviction in her voice was belied by the expression in her eyes. All right, she admitted with reluctant honesty, maybe sometimes in an unguarded moment she still felt the odd sharp tug of attraction for James. But in that she was hardly unique, she thought with dismissive confidence. There couldn't be many women who were completely immune to James's flagrant masculinity.

And it wasn't as if she'd never lived under the same

roof as a man before either. When she'd first moved to London she'd shared a large rented house perfectly harmoniously and platonically with flatmates of both sexes—much to her aunt's disapproval, she remembered with a grin.

Her grin broadened as she heard Timmy's gentle but quite distinctive little snore.

'That boring?' She pressed a kiss to his soft, rosy cheek and carried him back to his own room for his afternoon nap.

After settling him down in his cot, she made her way to the kitchen. Food! She was ravenous. Rummaging in the fridge for bread and cheese, she made a sandwich and ate it as she gazed out of the window that overlooked the rear, walled garden. The sunshine of the morning had gone and it was beginning to drizzle.

She started, glancing automatically at her watch, as she heard the front door open. What was James doing home this early? She frowned, hearing the exchange of male voices. There was someone with him.

Crossing to the door, she peeped out into the hall. James Fenner, a large box in his arms, was heading into his office, followed by three men she'd never seen before armed with a desk, a chair and a filing cabinet, all of which she had a feeling she might well recognise on closer inspection. Her eyes darkened suspiciously.

A few moments later the men emerged empty-handed, the three strangers smiling with satisfaction as James held out a wad of notes. A few seconds later the front door slammed.

Swiftly, Beth pulled out a chair and sat down with her plate.

'Beth?'

She swallowed a mouthful of sandwich. One. Two. Three.

'Beth?' The door flew open. 'Didn't you hear me?' James demanded.

She looked up at him innocently. 'Timmy's asleep,' she said pointedly. Formally dressed in a dark suit, his hair severely disciplined, James looked more familiar. But not reassuringly so, Beth thought with an uncomfortable dip of her stomach.

'Timmy'll sleep through anything,' James said airily.

Like last night, Beth mused.

'Snacking?' The blue eyes dropped to her now empty plate. 'I thought you'd get bored,' he said with satisfaction. Loosening his tie, he tossed it over the back of a chair.

'I'm far from bored, and this is the first chance I've had to have lunch,' Beth protested immediately.

He didn't appear to have heard her.

'If you're making tea...' He moved to the door.

'I wasn't, actually.'

'Bring mine through to my office.' He paused and glanced back over his shoulder. 'Please,' he added thoughtfully, as if experimenting with a new addition to his vocabulary, and disappeared down the hall.

A short time later, armed with a mug, Beth pushed open the office door. She placed the mug on James's desk, and then walked across the room to survey the recent arrivals. Just as she'd supposed—her desk, chair, filing cabinet and word processor.

'Surprised?' James was watching her with the smug complacency of a successful conjurer.

'So what's the temp doing? Sitting on the carpet with a notepad and pencil?'

'I couldn't find anyone suitable.' He shrugged. 'Or anyone who could make head or tail of your incomprehensible filing system,' he grunted. 'I spent most of the morning hunting down the Atkinson file.'

'It was in your in-tray...'

'So I discovered. Eventually.'

'Where you asked me to put it yesterday,' Beth completed pleasantly, sauntering towards the door.

'Beth!'

She looked back over her shoulder, gratified by the exasperation in his face. 'Yes?' she asked innocently.

'Off to have another snack? Watch the latest television soap?' The derisory note left his voice. 'I would like these letters dispatched before tomorrow, please,' he said quietly, and held out a cassette.

Beth hesitated and then, with an inward sigh, walked towards his desk and took the cassette.

'Timmy and I had made plans for the next few days,' she muttered, visions of the leisurely walks in the park disappearing. 'And we had social engagements,' she added, recalling Mrs Andrews' invitation.

'Plans?' James raised a sceptical eyebrow.

'We were going swimming...' she said defiantly. She had spotted a small, inflatable swimsuit amongst Timmy's clothes.

'Swimming?' James repeated thoughtfully, and confirmed what Beth had already guessed. 'Caro takes Timmy swimming sometimes. He loves it.' He paused. 'There's a pool in the basement. And a gym,' he added absently.

'You think Timmy might enjoy pumping iron too?' Beth enquired, her lips curving at the image forming in her head.

'Probably best to leave it another month,' James said gravely, and his own mouth twitched. The blue eyes sought and held hers for a brief second.

Swallowing hard, Beth walked over to her desk, switched on the word processor and loaded the cassette into the Dictaphone.

She looked up. 'I shan't hear Timmy if I use the earphones.' Aware of the growing gloom beyond the window, she stretched out an arm and flicked on the light switch.

'I'll listen out for him.'

As if on cue, the sound of a plaintive wail echoed down the hall.

'You get on with those letters,' James muttered, rising to his feet. 'He's completely out of routine,' he added accusingly, glancing at his watch.

Clicking on the Dictaphone, Beth watched him stride purposefully towards the door. 'He'll probably need changing,' she murmured sweetly to the broad, retreating back. Her eyes lit up with suppressed laughter as she saw him pause slightly before disappearing resolutely into the hall.

Her fingers began to move swiftly over the keyboard as she listened to the deep, articulate voice dictating fluently into her ear. So James couldn't find a suitable replacement? Try as she might, she couldn't help the tiny little glow of warmth. Though on second thoughts, she mused wryly, he probably couldn't find anyone rash enough to put up with him even temporarily.

She looked up, sensing James's presence instantly as he walked back through the door, carrying Timmy strapped into his portable reclining chair.

'Not there,' she protested, removing her earphones as he placed the chair in the middle of the carpet. 'He'll get a draught.'

'There aren't any draughts,' James said, but moved the chair over to the corner.

'Timmy won't be able to see what's going on there,' Beth objected.

Dark eyebrows drawn together in exasperation, James crossed to his desk, swept the papers to one side and placed the chair on top of it. 'Satisfied?' he enquired dryly, folding his long frame into his own chair.

Beth looked at Timmy, who was thoughtfully studying his pink bootees. Evidently deciding that they weren't to his taste, he tugged them off and deposited them casually on top of James's papers.

'Much better,' she agreed, fighting the gurgle of laughter as she surveyed the dark-haired man. James Fenner, tough, formidable, cynical, highly respected in the ruthless, cut-throat business world he inhabited, with a baby perched on the end of his desk and holding a pair of pink bootees absently in one lean hand. You're ruining your uncle's street cred, Timmy, Beth laughed inwardly.

Replacing the earphones, she forced her attention back to the screen in front of her, her eyes flicking from time to time across the room. Leaning back in his chair, James was studying the contents of a file, pausing occasionally to discuss some salient point with Timmy. Beth smiled, watching the hard features soften each time he turned to his nephew. So James Fenner wasn't totally invincible; he did have one tiny Achilles heel.

He had removed his jacket, the powerful shoulders clearly defined beneath the light blue shirt. Her mouth suddenly dry, Beth averted her eyes, stopping the cassette and rewinding the tape. Concentrate, she ordered herself, determinedly fixing her eyes on the screen.

After completing the last letter on screen, she printed them all out, checked them for errors and carried them over to James. He skimmed them swiftly, signed his name and handed them back to her.

'They should catch the last post if you hurry,' he told her crisply. 'There's a box just down the road on your left.'

Beth glanced unenthusiastically out of the window as she sealed the envelopes. Darkness had fallen, the flow from the street-lamps glistening on the cold, wet pavement below.

'I thought you country girls were as tough as old boots,' James said innocently, following her gaze. 'Didn't turn tail at a drop of rain.'

Without answering, Beth went to retrieve her raincoat from her bedroom, and as an afterthought stowed the letters in a small waterproof holdall. Tough as old boots! She slammed the door loudly as she departed from the flat and, ignoring the lift, pounded down the stairs. Pausing in the foyer to tuck her hair inside the collar of her coat and pull up her hood, she pushed open the door and, head bowed against the rain, walked hurriedly towards the post box.

It all happened so quickly that later Beth couldn't be sure whether the youth had appeared from behind her or had been waiting ahead in the shadows. One moment she was walking along the pavement, the next moment she was hurtling forwards, her arm almost wrenched from its socket as the holdall was torn from her grasp.

For a second she lay sprawled on the wet pavement, stunned and winded, every bone in her body jarred. This simply could not have happened to her. Disbelief gave way to an explosion of anger—anger that gave her the impetus to scramble to her feet. How dared he do that to her...how dared he...? Oblivious to her stinging hands, the painful throbbing in her left shoulder, she furiously retraced her route to the flat.

She fished out the key from her pocket, opened the door and then found her legs wouldn't move any further; they felt as if they were about to give way beneath her.

'Beth?' Having presumably heard her key in the door and been puzzled by her non-appearance, James emerged from the office. 'What the blazes...?' Eyebrows knitting together, he strode towards her.

'S-somebody snatched my b-bag with the letters in.' Her stiff, cold fingers fumbled with the buttons on her coat.

'What?' Incredulous blue eyes moved with concern over her ashen face and then hardened. 'Did he hurt you?' he demanded brusquely, a muscle tensing along the lean jaw.

'No,' Beth mumbled swiftly. 'I just l-lost my balance and slipped...' Or had she been pushed? For one fleeting second when she'd first seen the shadowy figure lurching towards her, before she'd realised that his only interest was in the bag, she had been so *scared*... She began to shake convulsively, and the next moment she was encircled by strong male arms.

'It's just delayed shock,' a deep voice murmured gently, soothing her as if she were Timmy.

But she wasn't a baby, and there was nothing remotely soothing about her immediate and wholly feminine awareness of that engulfing wall of solid male muscle. Beth froze, terrified that the slightest movement might inadvertently bring her even closer into the arc of the hard, lean body.

Her eyes were on a level with the firm, straight mouth. Why had she never noticed before just how sensuous the curve of that lower lip was? Warmth curdling in the pit of her stomach, she swiftly lowered her gaze so that it encompassed the unnerving expanse of tanned skin revealed at the V of the open-necked shirt. She could see the strong pulse beating at the base of his throat. Oh, God, hadn't she had enough shocks for one day?

'I'm all right now, James.' She forced the words through her dry lips, praying her desperation wasn't echoed in her voice. She thought he hadn't heard, could have sworn his hold on her tightened, and then, to her intense relief, his hands dropped to his sides.

'You're shivering,' he said abruptly. 'Go and have a bath and change into some dry clothes. I'll make a start on Timmy's tea.'

She nodded, avoiding looking directly up at him, and headed towards her room. Electing for a shower instead of a bath, she found her tension easing as she stood under the cascade of warm water. Slowly she began to grin. Being held in James's arms might not have been exactly comforting, but it had certainly been effective in banishing the earlier incident from her mind! Though she would have preferred slightly less disturbing therapy.

Drying herself swiftly, she tugged on a clean pair of jeans and a pink sweatshirt and headed back for the kitchen.

Timmy, a bib around his neck, was sitting in his chair on the floor, waving his small fists agitatedly as he watched his uncle remove a small tin from a mug of hot water and empty the contents into a red plastic bowl.

'It's all right. It's just coming,' Beth murmured reassuringly as she unstrapped him from his chair and sat down with him on her lap by the table.

'I telephoned the police.' James slanted a dark eyebrow at her. 'If you want to make a formal statement, you can drop in at the station in the morning.' He handed her the bowl.

'But a bag of stolen letters isn't exactly top priority?' Beth said dryly, surprised that he had even bothered to report it. She picked up the spoon, smiling as Timmy opened his mouth expectantly towards her like a ravenous fledgling. He obviously didn't need any coaxing.

She flicked a glance upwards, watching James prepare Timmy's bottle, his movements deft and economical.

'I'll leave it here to cool.'

Beth nodded and, expecting him to return to his office, was disconcerted when he pulled up a chair opposite her and sat down. Folding his hands behind his head, he stretched out his long legs indolently in front of him.

She tried to block him out, but was uneasily conscious of the blue eyes watching her every movement. What was he doing? Checking up on her feeding technique?

'That's your lot.' She scraped round the bowl and then grinned ruefully as Timmy lunged at the spoon, spattering the contents over himself. 'Keep working on the table manners,' she advised him, gently wiping his face and small hands.

Rising to his feet, James picked up the bottle of milk, checked the temperature and handed it to Beth before resuming his seat. Leaning back comfortably, Timmy began to suck tranquilly, his tiny hands fluttering against the bottle.

Beth's lips curved as they moved over his golden curls, feeling the warmth of his tiny body nestling trustingly against her breast. He was so small, so vulnerable, so totally dependent. Her arms tightened protectively about him.

'Do you want children, Beth?'

Beth was caught totally off guard by the unexpected question; her eyes jumped to the dark face. It showed no more than idle, passing curiosity.

'Maybe. Some day,' she said cagily. When—or if—she ever met a man with whom she wanted to spend the rest of her life.

'Career first, hmm?'

She shrugged as she placed the empty bottle on the table. That was not what she'd meant at all. Timmy looked up at her contentedly and gave a tiny yawn.

'Hard day at the office?' she murmured sympathetically.

'Probably be easier if I keep an eye on him while you prepare his bath,' James drawled casually as she rose to her feet.

'Probably,' Beth agreed gravely, and, moving across the floor, placed Timmy in his arms, hiding her grin until she reached the hall. You don't fool me for one moment, Mr James Fenner, she thought.

Glancing back over her shoulder as she reached Timmy's room, she saw James senior and James junior disappear into the lounge. No doubt by the time she returned Timmy would be fully au fait with the working of the London Stock Exchange, not to mention the Dow-Jones index.

She drew the bedroom curtains, laid out Timmy's nightwear and went into the *en suite* bathroom to fill his small baby bath. After placing a white fluffy towel on the radiator to warm, she made her way back to the lounge.

'James,' she began, pushing open the door, and faltered at the sight of the long, lean frame stretched out on the sofa. Timmy, safely cocooned between a hard shoulder and the back of the sofa, was flopped out beside him. Both were sound asleep.

Beth's eyes danced as she walked silently across the thick carpet. Who, she wondered, had put whom to sleep first? Reaching over James, she picked up Timmy, who mumbled protestingly and promptly fell back to sleep in her arms.

Pausing, Beth looked down at James. So he wasn't Superman after all. He looked younger, the lines of cynicism washed from his face, but even in sleep the angle of his square chin was tenacious. Her eyes moved over each strongly carved feature as if committing them to memory, lingering over the shadowed jawline and the firm, straight mouth. She swallowed hard. His hair was tousled and sprang across his forehead in the increasingly familiar waves. Suddenly grateful that her hands were fully occupied with Timmy, she turned away.

'I think we'll skip the bath until the morning,' she murmured softly as she entered his bedroom. Timmy fidgeted fretfully as she prepared him for bed, and then fell instantly asleep again as soon as she laid him in his cot. After dropping a kiss on his pink cheek, she tiptoed quietly from his room.

She peeped into the lounge, saw James hadn't stirred from his recumbent position and, humming quietly, returned to the kitchen.

Opening all the cupboards, she inspected the contents. James evidently liked pasta, which was fortunate because spaghetti bolognese and salad was one of her few culinary accomplishments. Gathering the ingredients, she set to work preparing the simple meal and was startled to discover just how inordinately happy she suddenly felt. She tended to stay on an even keel, and these swift mood changes were wholly out of character.

She set the table, placing the salad bowl in the middle, turned the heat low on the stove and, not pausing to analyze why, sped to her bedroom. Sitting down on her stool beside the dressing table, she brushed her hair over her shoulder and applied a light coat of lip gloss. Frowning slightly, she surveyed her reflection, disconcerted by the glow in her wide-spaced eyes, the wash of colour on her cheeks. She looked, she told herself forcefully, like someone who had been toiling over a hot stove, that was all...

James was still asleep when she entered the lounge, his deep chest moving up and down rhythmically.

'James.' Gently Beth shook his shoulder, instantly conscious of the hard muscle beneath her palm.

The long dark lashes flicked upwards, blue eyes moving slowly over her face.

'Beth,' he murmured softly, and smiled, the smile so unexpected that Beth's stomach dipped. 'Just mulling over the events of the day,' he informed her airily, swinging his long legs to the ground. 'Where's Tim?'

'I put him to bed while you were mulling over events.' Beth grinned. 'I've made some—' she began, her words drowned as James, glancing at his watch, cursed out loud.

'I've a taxi booked in twenty minutes!' He flung himself to his feet.

Beth looked at him disbelievingly. 'You're going out this evening?' she asked flatly.

He grunted something incomprehensible as he strode towards the door, and then paused, eyebrows drawn together. 'There's plenty of food in the kitchen. Help yourself to anything you want.'

She already had! Beth stared blankly at the empty doorway. So that was why James had been so insistent that she stay at the flat—as resident babysitter so that he could go out gallivanting every night. Oh, she didn't doubt for a moment that James was genuinely fond of his nephew—as long as Timmy didn't impinge on his social life.

She sped back to the kitchen and swiftly removed

the tell-tale second place setting. Then, turning off the pans, she drained the spaghetti and stared at the huge mound. How on earth was she going to manage to eat all that on her own? She'd be living off cold pasta for the rest of the week.

'Help yourself to anything you want,' he'd said. Opening the fridge door, she retrieved an open bottle of white wine she'd spotted earlier, poured out a glass and took a sip. It was ridiculous to feel so deflated, so disappointed. How exactly had she anticipated that she and James were going to spend the evenings at his flat anyway? she mocked herself. Enjoying cosy tête-à-têtes around the fire?

She piled spaghetti onto a plate, covered it in sauce and carried it over to the table with her glass. Determinedly she picked up her knife and fork, and laid them down again as James strode through the doorway in the process of knotting the red silk tie draped around his brilliant white shirt.

With growing disbelief his eyes moved from her laden plate to the mound of pasta still left in the colander.

'I'm hungry,' Beth said nonchalantly, immediately swallowing a mouthful with great relish. Uncomfortably aware of his continuing scrutiny, she looked up at him with irritation. It was not easy eating spaghetti with an audience.

'Will you be all right on your own with Timmy?' he asked quietly.

'Of course,' she said swiftly.

'Go easy on that.' Abruptly he indicated her glass of wine.

Beth nearly choked. What did he think she was planning? Some wild, solitary bacchanalian evening?

'Yes, James,' she said meekly when she could finally speak.

Turning on his heel, he disappeared into the hall. A few seconds later she heard the front door close behind him.

Beth stabbed at a piece of pasta with her fork, lifted it to her mouth and put it down again. Unbidden, the image of James gazing intimately across a candlelit table into the inviting eyes of Julia Summers unfurled in Beth's head.

She squashed it ruthlessly. How and with whom James chose to spend his leisure hours was of no concern or interest to her. But she was blowed if she was going to spend every evening babysitting on her own. Hadn't it occurred to James Fenner that she might have a social life too? One that she had no wish to put on hold just to convenience him!

CHAPTER THREE

'IS YOUR uncle always this nauseatingly cheerful first thing in the morning?' Beth enquired, sitting on the edge of the bed as she fastened the last button on Timmy's dungarees. 'And someone should tell him he's tone-deaf,' she added kindly.

As James's voice echoed around the flat, Timmy waved his small fists enthusiastically in the air.

'You're not going to be musical either,' Beth said sadly, and hugged him, drinking in the freshly bathed baby scent of him.

She had no idea what time James had arrived home last night, but, judging by his expansive mood at breakfast, he'd evidently had a successful evening. Of course, he might not have come home to the flat at all until early this morning...

She looked up as James strode into the room, dressed in a suit.

'You're not changed yet.' He glanced briskly at his wristwatch and then, stooping down, whisked Timmy off her lap.

Changed for what? Beth searched the dark face for a clue. Her jeans and red sweater seemed eminently practical for the day ahead. Wincing slightly, she rose to her feet.

'The board meeting,' James elucidated with exasperation as if she were being particularly dense on purpose. 'We should leave in ten minutes.'

44

'You're expecting me to attend the *board meeting*?'

'Well, who else is going to take the minutes?' James asked in the reasonable tone that never failed to infuriate her. He sauntered over to the window to show Timmy the view.

Dozens of other people! 'How about Sue?' Beth asked dryly, referring to James's second-in-command's PA, surveying the unresponsive back. It was odd how she could suddenly become indispensable when it suited him.

'And who's going to mind Timmy? Mrs Andrews?' James smiled blandly as he moved away from the window.

He wasn't serious, Beth thought in disbelief. 'You can't take Timmy to a board meeting!'

'He's looking forward to it,' he assured her briskly. Timmy beamed his endorsement.

'You can't...' Beth began again, her eyes flicking from the small golden head to the dark one, and stopped. The chairman and major shareholder of Stanton Enterprises could and would do whatever he chose. James could take half a dozen infants to the board meeting and she doubted whether anyone would dare demur.

'You haven't a baby seat in your car,' she reminded him hopefully, unconsciously flexing her left arm.

'Caroline left her car. We'll take that,' he said easily as they left the room. 'What's the matter with your arm? You didn't sprain it when you fell over yesterday, did you?'

'No.' She shook her head, registering his slight frown. Concern for her welfare or anxiety that she might not be fully functional? With a twinge of guilt she admitted that she was probably being unfair. 'My shoulder's just a bit stiff,' she said lightly. She seemed to have pulled a muscle, which had tightened up painfully overnight.

'By the way, did you manage to get all the letters reprinted last night?' James's brisk voice followed her down the hall.

What? Eyes sparking indignantly, Beth swung round to face him. 'No, I didn't,' she began heatedly. 'Timmy woke up twice, and...' Too late she saw the betraying twitch at the corners of the firm mouth. She grinned back weakly, suddenly wondering on how many other occasions over the past eighteen months she'd taken James seriously when he'd merely been teasing her—and risen straight to the bait.

'Bring the disk with you and I'll pass it on to Sue.'

Beth nodded and headed thoughtfully towards her room.

Fortunately the discomfort in her shoulder seemed to have eased as her muscles warmed up, she acknowledged thankfully a short time later as she sat in the back of the red saloon beside Timmy, clutching his baby bag on her knee. She'd just about had time to exchange her jeans for a serviceable blue skirt, but hadn't needed to witness the fleeting expression in James's eyes as she'd emerged from her room to be aware that her appearance fell far short of the immaculate, businesslike one she normally presented in the office. But then what had he expected, with him hammering on her door with a time-check every few seconds?

Tugging out a band from her jacket pocket, she

deftly tied her silky hair back in a pony-tail. How long was he going to keep up that incessant soft whistling?

'On balance,' she confided to Timmy as the car stopped at a set of traffic lights, 'I think I prefer the Pavarotti impersonation.'

The pavements were crowded with shoppers, pouring in and out of department stores that were festooned with decorations and fairy lights. Less than a week until Christmas, she reminded herself, and she still had no idea how she was going to spend the traditionally family occasion this year. If her parents hadn't been killed in that car crash when she was five; if she'd had siblings, or even cousins... She pulled herself up sharply. Christmas always brought out this self-pitying jag.

Her eyes flicked to James's head. His whole concentration was focused on the road ahead. He was a good driver, she acknowledged grudgingly—considerate to other road users, exhibiting an unexpected patience in the slow-moving traffic. It was the same patience he showed towards Timmy. In fact, it was only she who seemed to exasperate him so much at times.

Turning right into a car park in front of a large, modern office complex with the Stanton Enterprises logo prominent on the glass frontage, James drew into his reserved space. After switching off the engine, he strode round to the boot to retrieve the pushchair.

Timmy stared gravely up at the imposing building ahead as he was strapped into the buggy.

'Bit apprehensive, hmm?' Absently handing Beth his briefcase, James unselfconsciously began to push his nephew towards the entrance.

Picking up the baby bag with her free hand, Beth caught up with him as the automatic doors slid open in front of them. Had James felt apprehensive about attending his first board meeting? Her eyes flicked over the strong, assured male features. Somehow she doubted it. She doubted that James Fenner had ever felt insecure or uncertain in his life.

'Good morning, Mr Fenner.'

'Good morning, Anne.' As he propelled Timmy across the thick carpet, James seemed completely oblivious to the receptionist's startled, speculative gaze. But then, Beth mused wryly, he was probably so accustomed to commanding female attention, with or without his tiny appendage, that it no longer even registered with him.

Pausing by the Christmas tree placed prominently in the centre of the large foyer, he dropped to his haunches at the side of the pushchair, the tailored suit tautening across his broad back and muscular thighs. Ignoring the unwelcome dryness in her throat, Beth walked purposefully over to the lift and pressed the call button. Dratted hormones. She'd thought she'd finally managed to govern them, but they still caught her off balance when she was least prepared.

The lift doors opened, discharging a good-looking, fair-headed man.

'Beth.' He smiled warmly at her. 'I seem to have missed you the last couple of mornings.'

'Hello, David.' She smiled back at the young accountant with whom, owing to the proximity of their flats, she normally travelled to work on the underground.

'Still OK for tomorrow night?'

Beth cursed inwardly. She'd forgotten all about their casually arranged date.

'I'm sorry, David,' she began, and paused as she saw James looming within earshot. 'But I'll be a little late,' she finished brightly. 'Eight o'clock in the Red Lion?' She referred to a pub that lay equidistant between their two flats.

Nodding cheerfully, David greeted James with deferential respect, glanced curiously at Timmy and hurried away.

Knowing exactly why she'd changed her mind at the last minute when she'd fully intended cancelling her date with David Richardson, Beth explored James's face surreptitiously as he manoeuvred the pushchair into the lift beside her. With satisfaction she saw the dark eyebrows knit fleetingly across his forehead.

Good. It was about time he realised that her whole life didn't revolve around Stanton Enterprises and its chairman; realised that she hadn't been put on this earth solely for the benefit of James Fenner.

'Staff night off,' she said sweetly, meeting the disapproving blue eyes challengingly. Had she ruined his own plans for the following evening? she wondered hopefully. She looked down at Timmy, who was staring at her with unblinking eyes, their expression disconcertingly similar to his uncle's.

This really wasn't fair. She was outnumbered two to one.

All right, I'm being childish, she conceded. Retaliating for last night. But if she didn't stand up to James occasionally, even if it was just over a relatively minor issue, she'd be steam-rollered completely.

Two pairs of blue eyes continued to regard her in unnerving silence as the lift doors opened on the fifth floor.

'I'm entitled to some free time!' she muttered, shooting James a baleful glance.

'And that's how you normally spend your free time? With young Richardson?' he drawled, the lean, capable hands resuming their hold on the pushchair.

Young Richardson! The patronising amusement in the blue eyes—as if he found the whole idea of any man deliberately seeking and enjoying her company vastly entertaining—incensed Beth still further.

Timmy, evidently equally amused by the thought, began to chuckle.

This male bonding was going too far. Throwing them both a look of utter disgust, Beth stepped disdainfully out of the lift into the hushed luxury of the directors' domain and headed down the corridor to the well-appointed cloakroom. She hung up her jacket and retraced her steps, entering her own small office, now bereft of much of its furnishings. Leaving the baby bag in the adjoining kitchenette, she carried James's case through the connecting door to the plush, spacious office beyond, depositing it unceremoniously on the polished desk.

With Timmy in his arms, James was standing by the window with its panoramic view over the city, briefing his tiny, wide-eyed audience on the impending meeting.

Beth's lips curved involuntarily. Heaven help them if James ever had children of his own. They'd all probably suffer from executive stress by the time they were six months old. Her grin faded. The mental image of James with a wife, surrounded by dark-haired mini versions of himself, was one she suddenly shied away from.

'I'll go and check the boardroom,' she muttered at the broad shoulders, and headed swiftly back into the outer office. Armed with her notebook and a pile of papers, she made her way down the thickly carpeted corridor, past the small bedroom with *en suite* bathroom that James used occasionally, and the directors' dining room, to the boardroom at the far end.

After setting out a copy of the minutes of the last meeting and the morning's agenda in front of each chair drawn up to the oval table, she ensured that the carafe of water in the centre had been freshly replenished, and that the coffee-tray was ready on the sideboard beside the drinks cabinet.

Had James ever contemplated marriage, a family? With his low boredom threshold, Beth doubted he'd ever meet a woman who could hold his attention for longer than five minutes, let alone a lifetime. She drew up a chair to the right of the one at the head of the table, her usual position when taking minutes. His personal life seemed to mirror his working one—an endless quest for new challenges.

'Good morning, Beth.'

She looked up with a smile as the company secretary and financial director walked through the door, followed by three more dark-suited figures. After helping themselves to coffee, they sat down at the table.

Beth flicked a glance at their faces. None of them yes-men or puppets, they were all astute, well-paid professionals—and yet the minute James walked into the room they seemed to pale into insignificance.

'Good morning,' he greeted them briskly, the pushchair in front of him doing nothing to detract from his authority.

'My nephew,' he said laconically, positioning Timmy beside Beth, and, offering no further explanation, pulled up his own chair. But then when had James Fenner ever felt the need to explain himself to anyone? Beth mused, hiding her swift grin as she scanned the bemused expressions around the table. Just as she'd guessed, not one of them queried Timmy's presence or James's right to have him in attendance.

As James opened the meeting, Beth picked up her pencil, glancing at Timmy from time to time as her fingers skimmed over the pages in her notebook.

Reclining comfortably in his chair, Timmy was staring around with airy nonchalance, giving the occasional gurgle of approval when he heard his uncle's voice, evidently in total agreement with everything he said. Beth grinned. Crawler.

Without being dictatorial, James controlled the meeting with his habitual skill, encouraging discussion but quick to curtail the more verbose participants. As she listened to the deep, crisp voice, witnessed the respect on the faces of the men present, Beth could do nothing to stop the familiar surge of pride. A pride she had no right to feel, she reminded herself uncomfortably.

She adjusted her position slightly, and stiffened as she heard James give a brief résumé of the meeting he'd had the previous night with the managing director of the New York branch, who was in London on a flying visit. So James had been attending a business dinner last night, not enjoying a romantic candlelit one with Julia...

Beth was suddenly conscious of the blue gaze turned on her face, and wondered how on earth he had sensed her brief lapse in concentration when she hadn't even been directly in his line of vision.

'To recap...' he said shortly, his tone of voice informing her that he was not accustomed to repeating himself.

Her fingers tightening on her pencil, Beth swiftly jotted down the point she'd just missed, keeping her head studiously bowed until James drew the meeting to a close.

Confirming the time with a glance at the wall clock, Beth shut her notebook, checking the pushchair automatically as the directors began to file out of the room, dispersing towards their respective offices. Timmy's eyes were closed.

Gathering up his papers, James surveyed his small nephew. 'Deep in contemplation,' he commented sagely. He paused reflectively. 'Or he could just be asleep.'

'There is that possibility,' Beth agreed gravely, her stomach lurching as James's eyes locked with hers. She could deal with James Fenner, tough, hard-headed businessman, with relative equanimity, switch off. But how was she supposed to deal with this stranger with the strong, humorous face? How was she supposed to look into those dazzling blue eyes, alive with amusement, and feel nothing?

'Worn out by excitement,' he concluded solemnly,

and, rising to his feet, sauntered over to the sideboard. 'Coffee?' he enquired over his shoulder, evidently in no hurry to return to his office.

Having automatically risen to her feet when he had, assuming they were about to depart, Beth nodded and sat down again.

'Biscuit?' James proffered a plate as he placed her cup in front of her. 'It's all right—you can dunk it,' he drawled casually, resuming his own seat.

'I don't dunk—'

'You do when you think I'm not looking,' James cut in blandly. 'And when you tell little fibs, Ms Sinclair,' he continued mockingly, 'those tiny gold flecks in your eyes darken to brown.'

Disconcerted by both observations, Beth took a much needed gulp of caffeine and was further discomfited when James began to chuckle softly.

'What?' she enquired haughtily, completely oblivious to her moustache of frothy coffee.

'Here.' Stretching out a lean hand, he brushed her top lip with his thumb.

The physical contact was minimal, but so unexpected that it caught Beth completely off guard. Tiny little shock waves prickled down her stiffening spine, tingled to every nerve-ending in her body.

She was a fraction too slow in averting her tell-tale eyes, and glimpsed the comprehension in the equally revealing dark blue depths that told her as clearly as any words that James had not only noticed but was fully aware of the reason for her heightened colour.

Had she been equally transparent last night in his arms? Her fingers tightened around the coffee-cup, the heat in her face intensifying. Did it amuse James to discover that his slightest touch could reduce her to flustered adolescence? Or alarm him? Cringing inside, she swiftly drained the remains of her coffee, setting the cup down with a clatter as the tense silence was shattered by a sudden, ear-splitting bellow.

Visibly taken aback, James leapt to his feet and stared down at the buggy in disbelief. 'How can anyone that tiny make that much noise?'

Having successfully gained their attention, Timmy reduced his decibels to a plaintive whimper.

'Hungry?' Beth murmured sympathetically, rising to her feet and propelling the pushchair across the room.

'Of course he's hungry.' James opened the door and followed her out into the corridor. 'It's way past his lunchtime,' he grunted.

And whose fault was that? The implied criticism caught Beth on the raw.

'It wasn't my idea to force him to sit through a long, tedious meeting.' She groaned inwardly the moment the words, worthy of a peevish five-year-old, left her lips. What was the matter with her today? Heart sinking, she saw the blue eyes narrow.

'That's your view of board meetings, hmm? And do you find your job equally tedious?' James enquired silkily, pausing as they entered the outer office.

'Sometimes,' she lied perversely.

'In that case, perhaps you should think about looking for another job.'

'Perhaps I should,' Beth agreed, aping the cold, unemotional tone.

Icy blue eyes locked with frigid hazel ones, and then James turned on his heel and disappeared into the inner room. Refusing to even glance over her shoulder, Beth guided the pushchair into the kitchen.

'I don't even know what that was all about,' she confessed in bewilderment to Timmy as she filled up the kettle and removed a bottle of milk and a small tin from the baby bag.

'Won't be long. I'll just warm these up.'

'Boring' was the last adjective she would ever have used to describe working for James Fenner—so what had possessed her to profess otherwise? she wondered miserably.

'It's just coming,' she soothed as Timmy let out an anguished wail of desperation.

Swiftly she spooned the contents of the tin into a red plastic bowl, splattering some of it over her jumper in her haste.

'I should be wearing this, not you,' she said ruefully as she stooped down and fastened a bib around Timmy's neck. 'I'm just going to fetch a chair…won't be a sec…'

Unconvinced by her assurance, he began to roar his protest as she darted into the outer office to retrieve a hard-backed chair.

'Hello, Beth.'

Startled by the familiar husky voice, Beth swung round and saw the tall blonde, immaculately groomed in a coral-coloured suit, crossing the carpet towards her. She hadn't heard the door open, but then that was hardly surprising with Timmy at full throttle.

'Hello, Julia…coming, Timmy…' The scent of expensive perfume wafted over her.

'James in his office?' Green cat-like eyes surveyed Beth coolly.

Beth was saved the necessity of answering as the outer door was abruptly flung open.

'What exactly are you playing at, Beth? Hello, Julia.'

'What does it look like?' Beth snapped at the towering figure as she lifted the chair up. 'Rearranging the furniture, what else?'

Vaguely aware of Julia smiling up at James, murmuring something huskily about lunch, Beth swung away. The next second the chair was prised from her grasp. Carrying it with effortless ease, James strode into the kitchenette and placed it beside the fitted counter.

'Sit down!' he ordered as she followed him, and, unstrapping Timmy, placed him on her lap, sliding the bowl and spoon along the counter to within her reach. 'Think you can manage now?'

Mindful of his nephew's presence, Beth didn't answer. As she lifted the spoon towards Timmy, he turned his small face away fretfully.

Frowning, James picked up the empty tin and studied the label. 'Chicken and vegetables. He had that last night.'

Beth shot him an irritated glance. Didn't he have anything better to do with his time than oversee her? Like running an empire or two?

'This isn't an à la carte restaurant.' She'd picked out the tin at random from his kitchen cupboard. 'Set menu only.' Quickly she smiled reassuringly down into the small face. Weren't babies supposed to be very sensitive to atmosphere? she thought guiltily.

Timmy glared back up at her.

'Oh, he's so cute and cuddly.'

She had completely forgotten the other girl's presence, Beth realised as her eyes jumped to the blonde woman posed elegantly in the open doorway. And, judging from the expression on James's face, he had too—a fact that had evidently not gone unnoticed by Julia.

As the cool green eyes swept over her, Beth was disconcerted by the unmistakable hostility in their depths. Hey, it's not me upstaging you, she protested silently—it's a six-month-old infant. The cute, cuddly one.

'Come on, Timmy,' she coaxed gently again. But his small mouth remained stubbornly closed. Perhaps if his expectant audience disappeared it might help, she thought with renewed irritation. Timmy wasn't a variety act, and nor was she. The blue eyes continued to survey her balefully. What on earth had she done to deserve such censure? Beth pondered.

'Why don't you let me try?' Julia murmured.

Was she serious? Thoughtfully envisaging the coral suit tastefully daubed with liquidised chicken and vegetables, Beth obligingly vacated her seat and handed over Timmy. Nothing like a bit of audience participation.

'Oh, you are so adorable,' Julia informed him throatily, picking up the spoon.

To Beth's chagrin, his small face cleared instantly and, giving an enchanting smile, he devoured the proffered food with enthusiasm.

So Timmy had a penchant for blondes too! She flicked his uncle a swift glance from under her lashes. Leaning back against the sink unit, arms folded across his powerful chest, he seemed totally absorbed in the little tableau in front of him.

She could understand his preoccupation, Beth admitted. With Timmy sitting angelically on her lap, Julia, blonde and serenely beautiful, looked like a glossy advertisement for the perfect wife and mother. There was not a mark on either the bib or her suit.

'Would you hand me his bottle, please, James?'

Beth's muscles cramped involuntarily as she watched James smile down into the feline green eyes. Over the past two days Timmy seemed to have aroused a paternalism in him which she never would have suspected he possessed. Perhaps he had been equally surprised. Her gaze dropped back to Julia.

'Beth…'

Timmy, with his tousled golden curls, could easily be taken for Julia's son. Had that thought occurred to James too? Was he imagining Julia sitting there with their child on her lap?

'Beth!'

Startled, Beth's eyes jumped to James. The smile had gone.

'Telephone!'

Finally aware of the insistent ringing issuing from his office, Beth swung round.

'Whoever it is, I'll call them back.'

James's voice echoed after her as she sped into his office. Leaning across his desk, she picked up the telephone and dealt efficiently and courteously with the caller. After replacing the receiver, she walked back out of the office and paused, standing motionless for a moment as she gazed through the open kitchen doorway.

Their eyes locked over the top of Timmy's head, James and Julia were laughing together with easy, relaxed familiarity. Looking contentedly replete, Timmy joined in, gurgling happily.

'Mr Atkinson,' she said shortly as, his expression sobering, James raised a dark, quizzical eyebrow in her direction.

'Dan Atkinson?' he repeated, the last vestige of amusement disappearing from his eyes as he surveyed her. 'Why didn't you call me immediately?'

Beth's mouth tightened. 'Because you told me—' she began evenly.

'Oh, for Pete's sake, Beth,' he cut in. 'Surely you can use the occasional spark of initiative? You know perfectly well I spent the whole of yesterday morning trying to contact Dan.'

'How could I?' Beth asked icily as he strode past her. 'I wasn't here.' Her eyes followed his retreating figure as he disappeared into his office. Had he always been this unreasonable, this impossible to work for? Perhaps he'd been right earlier—perhaps it was time she started looking for another job...

'He needs changing.' Julia's cool, disdainful voice broke through her thoughts.

'He certainly needs something,' Beth agreed vehemently, startled to discover she had such an unlikely ally. She swung round, her sense of humour instantly restored when she saw the grimace on Julia's face as, with a tiny shudder, she rose to her feet and wordlessly deposited Timmy in Beth's arms.

Not so cute and cuddly any more, hmm? Beth hid her grin as she watched Julia glide out of the kitchen and cross the outer office towards James's open door.

There was a tiny snag in the back of the sheer stocking covering one long, shapely leg. Should she tell her? Beth wondered. It would be kinder not to, she decided virtuously, and, picking up the baby bag, slung it over her shoulder.

'Quick wash and brush-up,' she explained to Timmy as they headed along the corridor.

She attended to him with increasing dexterity and, kissing the top of his golden head, placed him carefully on the carpet. Running water into a basin, she swiftly splashed it on her face and grimaced at her reflection in the overhead mirror as she dried herself.

Despite her efforts to remove the stains, her sweater still showed evidence of Timmy's lunch, and her hair was escaping the confines of the pony-tail, silky tendrils trailing down her neck, waving around her face. She grinned. It was just conceivable, she conceded, that, in the sophisticated glamour stakes, Julia Summers might just have the edge today.

Tugging off the band, she shook her hair free, letting it tumble in a glossy mane to her shoulders. She had it trimmed regularly, but had worn it in much the same way since her teens. Perhaps it was time she had it restyled—maybe even thought about the odd blonde highlight.

She burst into laughter and, slinging the baby bag and her jacket over her shoulder, picked up Timmy, emerging into the corridor just in time to catch a glimpse of James and his blonde companion disappearing into the lift.

Well, that was just great. Without giving either her or Timmy a second thought, James had gone calmly swanning off to lunch with Julia.

'And what are we supposed to do?' She looked down into the small, upturned face as she headed into the office and through to the kitchenette. 'Hang around here for hours until he decides to remember our existence?'

Swiftly strapping Timmy into his pushchair, she wheeled him back through into the office. Perching on the edge of the desk, she picked up the telephone, punching in a familiar number. He could at least have had the courtesy to wait and tell her where he was going instead of just vanishing without a word.

'Wright Taxis.'

'Hi, Sally. It's Beth at Stanton Enterprises. Could I have a cab sent round as soon as possible? The usual account.'

'Hold on one sec...'

Beth's eyes darkened as they dropped to the pushchair. Was Timmy of no more importance to James than she was? Merely an amusing novelty of which he was already beginning to tire?

'Right. A cab should be there in ten minutes. Who's it for, Beth? Your gorgeous hunk of a boss? Now if I were ten years younger...'

'Make it twenty, Sal,' a male voice teased in the background.

Smiling wryly, Beth concluded the conversation and replaced the telephone. 'Your gorgeous hunk of a boss'.

'Pity the contents don't match the packaging, hmm, Tim?' She gave an inelegant snort. Not that James Fenner was a perfect Adonis by any means.

'There's a tiny bump along the bridge of his nose,' she informed his nephew. 'As if he's broken it at some time or other.' Perhaps one of her predecessors had been driven beyond endurance and had taken a swing at him, she mused thoughtfully. 'And when he smiles his mouth is slightly crooked.'

Grimacing slightly, she slid off the desk and rubbed her aching shoulder. 'And half the time he looks as if he needs a haircut.' Which he did, because he was always too busy to keep the appointments he asked her to make—and then cancel.

Wondering what Timmy was gazing at with such absorption, Beth glanced over her shoulder, jolting as she saw James leaning idly against the door jamb, watching her.

'What are you doing here?' she demanded without thinking, caught totally off guard by his appearance. He must have declined Julia's invitation and simply escorted her down to the foyer.

'This is my office,' he drawled dryly, sauntering towards her.

'I thought...' She shrugged, swiftly busying herself with Timmy as she pulled on his warm outdoor suit. How long had James been standing there listening? She frowned. There was something in the back of the dark blue eyes she didn't quite trust.

'Ready to go back to the flat? I'll just get the car keys.' He moved towards the inner office.

'There's no need to run us back,' Beth said evenly, slipping on her jacket. 'I've ordered a cab.' As well he knew. The infuriating, surprised innocence on his face as he swung round didn't fool her for one second.

'Why did you do that?'

'Because it was hardly fair on Timmy to keep him

hanging around here for hours waiting for you,' she said shortly.

'But he hasn't been,' James corrected her mildly.

'That is hardly the point, is it?'

'It isn't?' The blue eyes looked baffled. 'So what is the point?'

'The point is...' Beth's voice tailed off, her eyes dilating with appalled horror as she finally faced the unpalatable truth, the point was she'd been jealous of Julia. She hadn't ordered the taxi out of concern for Timmy's welfare, she recognised with burning shame—warm and fed, he would have been perfectly content to remain in the office—but in order to make some stupid, illogical protest.

'Taxi'll be here any minute,' she muttered, desperate to escape the observant, astute blue eyes. And, taking hold of the pushchair, she propelled it swiftly out of the door and sped towards the waiting lift.

She'd watched numerous women flit in and out of the office and James's life with complete equanimity over the past eighteen months, so why, out of the blue, had she experienced that most destructive of emotions today? Unhappily, Beth punched the button for the ground floor. All those months of convincing herself that she had built up complete immunity to James had been just an illusion. Right now, she felt as vulnerable as she had in those first few weeks when she'd begun working for him.

'Back to square one,' she muttered resignedly, and then grinned weakly down at the pushchair. 'You know that you're responsible for this, don't you?' she murmured with mock severity. It was seeing James with Timmy, witnessing his gentleness, his patience, his strong male protectiveness that had so unsettled her.

'I don't always like the chairman of Stanton Enterprises,' she said slowly. 'But the trouble is, it would be very easy to like your uncle James.' She paused uneasily. 'Rather too much.'

And therein lay the danger. Feeling the occasional tug of physical attraction towards James Fenner was one thing—but becoming emotionally drawn to him would be catastrophic.

Grateful that the receptionist was engaged on the telephone, saving the necessity for conversation and the inevitable interrogation about Timmy, Beth positioned herself just inside the door until she saw the taxi draw up.

The grey sky of the morning had given way to a clear blue one, the sun's rays surprisingly warm for December, she noticed absently as she emerged into the open air.

Greeting her cheerfully, the taxi driver helped her into the back of the cab with Timmy, making sure that they were both securely strapped in before folding up the pushchair and stowing it on the floor.

'Where to?' he enquired, turning his head as he returned to the driver's seat.

'South Kensington, please.'

'St James's Park.' A deep, authoritative voice overrode hers as the passenger door was tugged open and James slid into the seat beside her.

'Yes, sir.' The driver responded immediately and without question, and by the time Beth had gathered her wits the glass partition had been closed and the cab was moving smoothly into the street.

CHAPTER FOUR

BETH was incensed. Her eyes jerked from the driver to James. How typical of him to commandeer her taxi and countermand her instructions without any explanation whatsoever. Equally infuriating was the way the driver had obeyed him so promptly without seeking any confirmation from her first.

'Stop scowling, Beth. You'll get frown-lines.' Idly James stretched out his legs more comfortably in front of him. 'And you're frightening Timmy.' He gave her a bland smile.

Beth ignored it. How could she have seriously thought for one moment that she might be in danger of falling for this man? OK, he might have a soft spot for his nephew. OK, he might have the most devastatingly blue eyes she'd ever seen in her life. But so what? She was sick to death of his arrogant high-handedness, sick to death of being treated as if she was of no significance at all.

'Oh, for heaven's sake, Beth, have a sandwich,' James drawled. 'You always get tetchy when you're hungry.'

If she was feeling tetchy it was perfectly justifiable. What sandwich? Suspiciously she watched as he delved into the recesses of his dark overcoat then tossed a carrier bag onto the seat between them.

'You hijacked my taxi because you had a sudden whim to go on a picnic? In December?'

'Time Timmy had some fresh air,' he said laconically, and added reprovingly, 'He was cooped up in the flat all day yesterday.'

Beth opened her mouth, and shut it again swiftly as she saw the glint in his eye. She wasn't going to walk into that little trap again, she thought determinedly as she inspected the contents of the carrier— whatever the provocation. Somehow she just couldn't quite believe that James had elected for an alfresco sandwich and the company of a six-month-old infant in preference to dining in salubrious surroundings with a beautiful blonde who was clearly besotted with him.

'They're all the same,' he murmured wearily.

'Blondes?' Had he begun to tire of Julia the way he had all her predecessors? She was startled by her immediate rush of sympathy for the other girl—for all the women who had been rash enough to get involved with him.

'What?'

'Oh, the sandwiches.'

James was looking at her as if she were deranged.

'Very democratic,' she observed swiftly.

'Merely expedient. One less thing for you to argue about.'

Beth shot him a look from under her eyelashes.

'Do you know the reason why I employed you?' he suddenly asked. 'Not because you were better qualified than any of the other applicants, but because I thought you'd be peaceful to have around.' He shook his head in disbelief. 'Peaceful!'

'You mean what you wanted was a devoted, loyal, selfless little mouse who would spend the next forty years of her life scurrying around after you without complaint?' Beth enquired sweetly. And she had been that little mouse for the first few months, Beth acknowledged with disgust. A ridiculous, starry-eyed little mouse.

'Well, naturally,' James drawled. 'The perfect secretary.' His mouth twitched. 'So, how the hell did I end up with you?'

'Good fortune?' Beth suggested. Expecting James's immediate retort, she was surprised when he remained silent, the blue eyes unreadable as they rested on her face. Was his silence a tacit admission that he agreed with her, accepted that she was highly competent at her job?

Huh! Well, about time too, she thought with satisfaction, and peeped into the second bag in the carrier. 'Breadcrumbs?' she murmured with wide, innocent eyes.

'For the ducks,' he said loftily.

'Of course.' Her lips curved. Why else would the chairman of a huge, multi-national company be carrying breadcrumbs in the pocket of his expensive overcoat? Acutely conscious of the long, sprawling limbs only inches away from her own in the confined space, Beth thoughtfully envisaged the catering staff's reaction to James's imperious demand for two sandwiches and a bag of breadcrumbs. At the double.

'Look out the window, Timmy, and you'll see Buckingham Palace on your right,' James instructed as the cab approached the park and drew to a halt.

Unimpressed, Timmy continued to stare up in fascination at the hand strap swaying gently above his head.

'I don't think he's quite mastered his left from his right yet,' Beth offered pensively, looking down into the small, absorbed face as James reached for the door handle. Unstrapping Timmy, she zipped up his suit and passed him carefully out of the taxi into James's waiting hands.

'Oh, you greedy little pigs,' Beth admonished two colourful drakes as she leant over the bridge, trying to distribute her handful of breadcrumbs fairly. 'Give the others a chance.' Flicking her hair back over her shoulder, she grinned up at James, who was standing by her side with Timmy held firmly in his arms.

'Throw it in the water,' he instructed his nephew. Inspecting the tiny morsel of bread in his hand, Timmy beamed gratefully and popped it in his mouth.

Beth's grin widened as she turned her head, admiring the picturesque view of the lake with Buckingham Palace in the background. Then, swinging round, she looked down towards Horse Guards Parade, and Whitehall beyond.

She still hadn't explored London fully, she realised with a pang of guilt, watching a group of tourists meandering by the lake, cameras at the ready. But then, she mused without rancour, watching James as he deftly put Timmy back in his chair, with the increasing number of weekends she'd been working, when had she had the time?

'One sandwich left,' she murmured, producing it from the carrier as they sauntered on over the bridge.

'Half each?' James raised a quizzical eyebrow. 'Unless you feel like being totally altruistic?'

'Nope,' she said cheerfully, handing him his portion, smiling inwardly at the sheer incongruity of wandering around a London park with the immaculately tailored chairman of Stanton Enterprises, pushing a pram and eating half a sandwich.

Even stranger, she realised, giving James a sideways glance as he paused by the water's edge, was the fact that it seemed like the most natural thing in the world to be here with him. She couldn't remember ever feeling so relaxed and at ease in his company, feeling so pleasurably aware of him with no sense of constraint or tension. With amusement she saw two middle-aged women turn their heads as they passed by—not for a second glimpse of the enchanting occupant of the pushchair, but of the towering man by her side. Was no woman immune to him?

As the breeze from the lake ruffled his thick hair, he raked back an errant lock with his hand, the impatient gesture now so familiar that her heart squeezed.

'Need a haircut,' he muttered half under his breath. 'As I apparently do most of the time.'

She grinned, oddly unperturbed by the confirmation that he had definitely overheard her earlier soliloquy. 'Look, Timmy, here are some more ducks swimming towards us.' She fished in her pocket for the bag of breadcrumbs.

Timmy yawned.

'He was hoping we were going to take him to a museum or gallery,' James explained, looking sympathetically at his nephew.

'Or a conducted tour of the Stock Exchange or Houses of Parliament,' Beth added understandingly, taking a handful of breadcrumbs before passing the bag to James.

'Haven't done this for years.' His eyes were a brilliant, unclouded blue as he aimed a bread pellet. 'I'd forgotten just how therapeutic it is.'

Therapeutic? Beth surveyed his profile thoughtfully. Did the pressure of running a huge empire, the constant decision-taking, the knowledge that he was directly and indirectly responsible for hundreds of people's livelihoods ever take its toll on him? Her eyes rested on the resolute, uncompromising angle of his jaw, the tenacious set of his square chin, and she shook her head dismissively. No. He took it all in his stride, thrived on the cut and thrust of the ruthless world he inhabited. She smiled. It took a six-month-old baby to knock James Fenner off balance!

Conscious of the lowering sun, she stooped to check that Timmy was warm enough.

'He'd survive the Arctic in that get-up,' James observed as they carried on along the path. 'Fancy a cup of tea somewhere?'

'And a sticky bun?' Beth grinned her acceptance, suddenly feeling absurdly and ridiculously happy. She didn't want the afternoon to end; she wanted to hold on to this unexpected and new-found comradeship with James for as long as possible. She could even tolerate his whistling, she thought, unable to suppress a giggle as he began a slightly off-key rendition of an old sea shanty.

He stopped whistling and quirked an eyebrow. 'That bad, hmm?'

'That bad,' Beth agreed. In a clear, sweet voice she

sang the words to the first line. 'It goes down a note at the end, not up.'

'Like this?' He tried to sing.

'Um, not quite like that,' Beth admitted as his voice died away, and burst into laughter at his crestfallen expression.

'You know what really hurts?' he confessed. 'My mother's a music teacher and my father was a professional musician until he retired.'

As her laughter died away, Beth looked up at him, intrigued. She had never once heard him mention his parents before. 'I didn't even know you had a mother and a father,' she mused aloud, unthinkingly.

'It is fairly normal,' he said dryly, and then cursed under his breath. 'I'm sorry, Beth. That was crass of me.' He frowned, walking on in silence for a moment, and then asked quietly, 'Do you still miss your parents?'

'I don't really remember them,' she said evenly, deliberately keeping her expression impassive.

And that was perhaps what saddened her most—that she'd never even had a chance to know them as people. Instead throughout her childhood she'd built up an idealistic picture of them in her imagination as the perfect parents, who, had they lived, would have given her all the love and understanding her aunt had failed to do.

It doubtless hadn't been easy for her father's sister to have a child suddenly foisted on her, and Aunt Mary had fed, clothed and educated Beth. But she still found it very hard to feel any genuine affection for the woman who had made it abundantly clear all those years ago that she regarded her small, bewildered niece as no more than an unwelcome duty.

Grateful that James made no attempt to pursue the subject, she flicked him a quick glance, slightly disconcerted by the thoughtful, speculative expression in his eyes as they rested on her face. Perhaps her expression had unwittingly revealed more than she'd intended, she thought uneasily, and resolutely pushed the past to the back of her mind.

Timmy, she noticed, was almost asleep, his blue eyes glazing over as his eyelashes flickered downwards. She frowned. 'Why didn't Caroline leave Timmy with your mother?' she asked with sudden curiosity. It seemed far more logical for him to stay with his grandmother than a bachelor uncle.

'My parents have flown over to the States to spend Christmas with my eldest sister,' he explained casually. 'Her husband's based there for a couple of years.'

'Your eldest sister?' She'd assumed that Caroline was his only sibling.

'I've five sisters. All younger than me.'

'Five?' she echoed in disbelief.

'Caro, Sarah over in the States, Anna, who's a concert pianist, and the twins, Ruthie and Becky, who are still at college.' He raised an eyebrow. 'Studying...'

'Music?' Beth finished, and grinned as he gave an assenting nod, fascinated by the knowledge that he had grown up as part of a large and—judging from the warmth in his eyes when he spoke of them—close-knit and affectionate family. The very thing she'd once craved more than anything else in the world.

She looked up into his strong, assured face, watching the expression on it as he looked down into the pushchair to check on Timmy's welfare. Big brother. It was a role in which she would have had difficulty casting him a few days ago, but now it was one she could easily see him fulfilling.

She could imagine him as a boy, teasing his younger sisters unmercifully, occasionally losing patience with their more feminine pursuits but above all being fiercely protective of them. And the fact that one of his sisters had entrusted her small, precious son to him without a qualm spoke volumes about his adult relationship with them.

'Sarah was the one responsible for this.' His eyes teasing her, he indicated the slight bump on his nose. 'Whacked me with a cricket bat when she was six.'

'I expect you deserved it,' Beth said severely. Had he overheard everything she'd said?

Her eyes dropped to his hands grasped lightly around the handles of the pushchair, absorbing the long, supple fingers that wouldn't have looked amiss spanning a keyboard. Had he ever resented not inheriting his parents' talent as his siblings had? Was that what had motivated him to succeed in such a completely different field from the rest of his family? Beth grinned to herself. Somehow the image of frustrated, embittered musician wasn't one that quite fitted James Fenner.

'Incidentally,' James drawled casually by her side, 'do you really find board meetings tedious?'

Beth stiffened in disbelief. Did he really have to drag that up again? And now, of all times? 'I shouldn't have said it...' she muttered, and stopped as she saw the suspicion of a smile tugging at the corners of the straight mouth.

'So do I sometimes!' he confessed, turning his head to look down at her.

'You do?' Beth grinned at him incredulously.

'But that, Ms Beth Sinclair, is in absolute confidence!'

'Of course, Mr James B. Fenner,' she assured him primly, the laughing blue eyes beginning to make her feel dizzy. James B. Fenner. How many times had she typed out those words? And she still didn't have a clue as to what his second name was. There was just so much about this man she didn't know, she thought with a sudden, aching sense of loss.

As they exited the park opposite Horse Guards Parade, Beth glanced absently at her watch and came to an abrupt halt.

'James!' she said urgently. 'Andrew Harrison has an appointment with you in half an hour.'

He ground to a stop beside her, eyebrows knitted across his forehead. 'Dammit all, Beth, why didn't you remind me earlier?'

'Because I forgot too!' She wasn't a computer, and hadn't had access to his desk diary for the last two days. And when did James ever need reminding about a business appointment anyway? It was unheard of for him simply to forget!

'What a ridiculous time to have a meeting,' he growled as, handing the pushchair to Beth, he stood on the edge of the pavement, his eyes narrowing as he scanned the traffic. 'Last thing in the afternoon, a few days before Christmas.'

Beth hid her grin. Andrew Harrison, the managing

director of a recently acquired subsidiary, had been of the same opinion when she'd originally organised the meeting—at James's insistence.

'You and Timmy take this back to the flat,' he ordered as he flagged down a cab, 'and I'll grab another one and go direct to the office.'

Beth flicked him a quick glance as she heard the unmistakable reluctance in his voice. Was he regretting that the afternoon had to end so abruptly too? Hey, don't read too much into the fact that just occasionally even a workaholic can feel like playing hookey for a few hours, she warned herself. And don't forget who's the star attraction, she added, lifting Timmy out of his chair and cradling him gently in her arms.

But it had been nice, she mused wistfully as the cab drew away, to have felt, if only for a short time, not like James's employee but like a woman whose company he was actually enjoying rather than just tolerating. Craning her neck, she looked out of the back window at the tall, solitary figure remaining behind on the pavement. Or was that just wishful thinking?

'Feel better now?' Beth murmured as Timmy drained the last drop of milk from his bottle. She wiped his mouth, untied his bib and, rising to her feet, carried him out of the kitchen and across the hall to the lounge.

Flicking on the wall lights, she set him down carefully on his brilliantly coloured activity mat, smiling at the enthusiasm with which he immediately started patting the assortment of padded animals that squeaked and rattled beneath his exploring fingers.

'I think I like the elephants best,' she decided, walking across the thick carpet to the French windows. She stifled a yawn, realising for the first time just how tired she was. 'Especially the one with the big red sun-hat.' Pausing for a moment, she gazed out beyond the shadowy balcony to the glitter of lights in the distance. Was James still at the office? Or was he at this very minute sitting in the car heading homewards?

Humming softly, she turned away and sat down on the carpet beside Timmy. Leaning back against the sofa, she stretched her jean-clad legs out in front of her, her ears tuned all the while for the sound of a key in the front door.

Her head jerked upwards, her pulse rate accelerating. Was that him now?

The firm footsteps in the hall were unmistakable, as was the deep, commanding voice.

'Beth? I'm home.'

'The lord and master's returned.' She grinned at Timmy. 'We're in the lounge,' she called out, and could do nothing to stop her rush of pleasure as James strode through the door.

'So this is how you both spend your time when I'm not here,' he drawled with mock severity.

'Lounging around,' Beth agreed, her heart missing an unsteady beat as she met the teasing blue eyes.

'I like the elephants, Tim.' Loosening his tie, James surveyed his beaming nephew. 'Especially the one with the red sun-hat,' he added thoughtfully, and lifted an enquiring eyebrow as Beth gave a snort of laughter.

'Nothing,' she denied, shaking her head. The room

seemed to have diminished in size and become charged with an infectious energy that instantly dispelled her weariness. 'Come on, Timmy. Time for bed.' A little cautiously she scrambled to her feet.

'Here.' James abruptly reached into the pocket of his jacket. 'Picked it up on the way home,' he added laconically, handing her a small bag with a chemist's logo on the front. 'Should help.'

Frowning with puzzlement, Beth opened the bag and then looked up, startled, as she extracted the small tube of muscular rub. How had he known her shoulder was hurting her when she'd been suffering in a dignified silence all day?

'Go and put some on now,' he ordered. 'I'll get Tim ready for his bath.' Tossing off his jacket, he rolled up his sleeves, and, stooping down, picked up his nephew.

'Right. Thanks.' Pretending to be engrossed in the instructions on the tube, Beth headed out of the door, bursting into laughter when she reached her room and caught a glimpse of her reflection in the mirror. From that idiotic expression on her face, anyone would think James had just showered her with red roses, not a tube of rather dubious-smelling salve.

She wrinkled her nose as she applied some to her left shoulder, and grinned. Not exactly Chanel, was it? She tugged her sweater back over her head, conscious that the warmth tingling through her wasn't solely attributable to the hastily administered cream. She darted into the bathroom to wash her hands, taking the opportunity to run a comb through her hair. After sweeping it back over her shoulders, she flicked off the bedroom light as she passed through it, and went in search of James.

She discovered him sitting on the bed in Timmy's room, attempting to dry the uncooperative, wriggling infant on his lap—who had evidently had the quickest bath on record.

'Keep still, Timothy,' James commanded.

Ignoring him, Timmy continued to battle defiantly against the towel, thrashing his tiny fists and feet furiously in the air.

Was she imagining it, Beth mused, watching with interest from the doorway, or did James Fenner actually look just the tiniest bit harassed? It must certainly be a novel experience for him to have an order flouted so blatantly.

'He nearly fell asleep in the bath.' Looking nonplussed, James surveyed his writhing, squirming nephew.

'He's over-tired,' Beth said in her best, briskly efficient nanny voice, savouring the look of relief on James's face as he speedily transferred Timmy to her waiting arms.

'You've had a busy day, haven't you?' Beth said softly, smiling into the fretful pink face. 'No wonder you're tired.' Engrossed in soothing her small charge as she prepared him for bed, she was temporarily oblivious to everything else, completely unaware of the thoughtful dark blue eyes concentrated on her absorbed face.

Kissing his velvety cheek, she laid Timmy down in his cot, tucking him up carefully as his golden lashes began to flicker downwards. For a moment she stood watching him in silence and then turned away, cannoning straight into James.

She must have caught him completely off balance, because as she instinctively grabbed hold of his shoulders to steady herself he caught his foot on the bedside rug and they both toppled sideways, landing in a jumbled heap on the divan.

For a second Beth couldn't even think straight, let alone speak, aware only of the hard male body sprawling against her. Her leg had somehow become trapped between his; she could feel every sinew and muscle through her jeans. James's face was only inches away from hers—she could see her reflection in his dark eyes, feel the warmth of his sharply expelled breath on her skin.

'My God, Beth, ever thought of taking up rugby? With a tackle like that...' James muttered gruffly as he disentangled himself and rose jerkily to his feet.

'You shouldn't have crept up behind me like that,' Beth muttered back, scrambling upright. Her legs felt like candyfloss, and she had the strongest suspicion that her face was glowing like a beacon. Glancing at the cot to check that Timmy hadn't been disturbed, she followed James from the room. 'And that rug is downright dangerous. What if either of us had been holding Timmy and tripped up?'

'Well, we weren't!' James growled over a broad shoulder as he strode down the hall.

'I'm going to move it first thing in the morning.' Beth glowered at the retreating, towering figure.

'You do that!' he grated, flinging open the kitchen door. 'And while you're at it, with your propensity for falling over and bumping into everything in sight, why don't you clear the whole damn room of furniture?' Coming to a halt, he swung round so abruptly that Beth almost collided with him again.

'Why are we arguing?' he demanded, his eyebrows drawn in a black line as he looked down at her. 'About a damn mat?'

'I don't know,' she mumbled, slipping onto a chair by the table. They must have sounded like a couple of bickering four-year-olds, she thought weakly. Except, she registered with a frisson of unease, that ridiculous little explosion hadn't erupted over a mere bedside rug.

She watched as James wordlessly reached in the fridge for a bottle of wine and poured out two glasses. Handing her one, he pulled up a chair and sat down opposite her.

'Truce?' He quirked an eyebrow as he raised his glass.

'Truce,' Beth agreed, not quite able to match his flippant tone as the blue eyes caught and held hers across the table. Determinedly breaking his gaze, she took a sip from her glass and frowned, her nose wrinkling as for the first time she registered the tantalising aroma pervading the kitchen.

'Chicken casserole,' James drawled as her eyes moved to the stove. 'Just a little something I prepared earlier,' he added modestly.

Tension easing, Beth's mouth curved. 'Mrs Andrews? And an automatic timer?'

'They may have helped,' he conceded with a grin. Taking another sip of his wine, he rose unhurriedly to his feet. 'I'm just going to have a quick shower and change, if you'd like to set the table.'

With a small sigh of contentment, Beth placed her knife and fork together on her empty plate. She felt warm and relaxed, enveloped in a rosy glow of well-being induced by good food and, she admitted, smiling across at James, even better company. His conversation had been light, amusing and undemanding, the occasional silences falling between them unstrained and comfortable.

James smiled back at her. 'Fruit? Cheese and biscuits?' he offered lazily.

'I don't think I could eat another thing,' Beth confessed. 'You're an excellent cook,' she teased him gently, wondering wistfully why their relationship couldn't always be this easy.

'Shall we have coffee in the lounge?' Standing up, James reached for the hot percolator and set it on a tray.

'OK.' A little reluctantly, Beth pushed herself to her own feet and added two cups and saucers to the tray.

'While you're there, could you dig out a loaf of bread from the freezer?' James asked as she extracted the milk from the fridge. 'We'll need it for the morning.'

Nodding, Beth lifted the lid of the freezer, her eyebrows shooting up as she surveyed the contents. 'Do you happen to like fruitcake by any chance?' she asked, looking up at James incredulously. 'The freezer's absolutely stashed with them.'

'Is it?' He looked at her uneasily. 'Um, how many exactly?'

'Seven—no, eight.' Had she discovered his secret vice? she wondered, suppressing a gurgle of laughter. 'And there could be another one lurking at the bottom.' Shaking her head in disbelief, Beth unearthed a loaf of bread and closed the lid.

'Nine?' He blanched visibly as he picked up the jug of coffee and moved to the door. 'My mother keeps making them,' he said resignedly. 'Apparently I used to love home-made fruitcake when I was about twelve, and now every time I see her...'

'She bakes you a cake?' Beth snorted with laughter as she saw the expression on his face. Carrying the tray, she followed him out of the kitchen and into the lounge.

'It's my own fault,' he muttered. 'I really ought to tell her, but...'

'It requires tact and diplomacy?' Beth suggested innocently. She set the tray down carefully on the low table by the sofa and sat down at one end.

'Something like that,' he agreed, the straight mouth twitching at the corners as he handed her the coffee-jug. Moving across to the French windows, he stood looking out at the lights of the city, and then drew the curtains.

'Have you always lived in London?' Beth asked idly as she poured out the coffee.

'I was brought up in Kent, just outside Canterbury,' he answered casually, joining her on the sofa. He crossed one lean, powerful leg over the other, resting his foot on the opposite knee. 'But except for a brief period in Winchester when I was married I've been based in London for most of my adult life. I dislike commuting.'

Beth barely heard his last observation, staring up at him with wide, startled eyes. 'I didn't know you'd been married.'

CHAPTER FIVE

SEEMING oblivious to the shock in Beth's voice, James shrugged casually. 'It was a long time ago,' he said easily.

For a moment she thought he wasn't going to continue, and then he turned towards her, leaning back against the arm rest, and added quietly, 'I made a mistake, Beth.'

A mistake he had no intention of ever repeating. With a tiny chill, Beth read the unspoken message in the back of the shadowed blue depths.

Then, inexplicably, James began to laugh softly. 'Will you stop gazing at me like that with those huge, tragic dark eyes?' Gently he touched her upturned face. 'I was very young, and undoubtedly at the time my male ego took a bit of a battering, but that was all. No lasting damage.'

Warmth bubbling through her from the fleeting caress, Beth smiled back, masking her scepticism. Whatever his protestations to the contrary, however lightly he might dismiss his marriage, she didn't believe for one moment that he had walked away from it unscathed.

'I had a call from Caroline just before I left the office,' James murmured, reaching for his coffee.

'Did you?' Beth said absently, slightly surprised he hadn't mentioned it earlier. The subject of his marriage, she registered, was now firmly closed; the ques-

tions whirling around in her head, even if she dared
ask them, were never to be answered.

But, try as she might, it was impossible not to wonder about the shadowy, faceless woman whom James
had once loved enough to commit himself to her completely. Beth's stomach gave an uncomfortable little
flip. A commitment he was never going to risk making again.

'Mike's responding well to treatment, but it looks
as if he's going to be in hospital for another couple
of weeks, and then he'll probably need a week to ten
days' convalescence before he's fully fit to travel.'

'Caroline's not going to be back for nearly a
month?' Beth jolted. A few more days she could cope
with. Maybe a week. But seeing James first thing in
the morning, over breakfast, with his hair still damp
and tousled from the shower, and last thing at night,
watching him with Timmy, sharing his home—for another month?

'I've a week's leave just after Christmas.' She
avoided his eyes.

'Postpone it.'

'Like I have the last three times?' she enquired
dryly. In the same way that she'd cancelled so many
of her weekend plans. And on each occasion, despite
her obligatory protest, she'd never really minded, had
she? The admission disturbed her.

Summoning every ounce of will-power, she forced
herself to meet his gaze squarely. 'I'm sorry, James,
but...' Her voice trailed off.

'But?' he prompted. Replacing his cup and saucer
on the table, he leant back, resting an arm along the

top of the sofa behind her head. 'You don't still doubt you're competent to mind Timmy, do you?'

Of all the gall! 'No, I don't,' she denied immediately, and saw from the glint in his eyes that she'd fallen headlong into the baited trap yet again.

'Because you've passed your trial period quite satisfactorily.'

Beth swallowed, the warm, teasing blue eyes beginning to mesmerise her. It wasn't her competence in dealing with Timmy she doubted.

'So that's settled, hmm?' he said softly.

'Yes,' she mumbled weakly, acutely conscious that his hand had dropped to her shoulder and was gently kneading the stiff muscles. Slow, hypnotic warmth seeped through her.

'Did the salve help?'

'Mmm.' She was enveloped in a languorous, soporific bubble of unreality. It would be so easy to let her head drop against that hard chest, to curl her arms around his neck. Her half-closed eyes moved over the strong planes of the dark face and rested on the hard, straight mouth. It would be so easy just to reach across those few short inches...

Desperately she fought her way back through the haze to full consciousness, to sanity.

'More coffee?' she enquired brightly, and was about to lean forward when she felt James's hand tighten on her shoulder.

'Listen!' he said softly.

The only thing she could hear was the thudding of her own heart. 'Timmy?' she said instinctively.

He shook his head and, springing to his feet, reached for her hand and pulled her upright.

'James!' she protested as he propelled her across the room. Was he on some sort of fresh air kick? she wondered in disbelief as, releasing her hand, he swiftly drew aside the curtains and flung open the French windows, cold night air rushing into the room. And then she heard it. The sound of a brass band and joyous voices raised in song.

'It's an open-air carol service!' she said with delight, stepping out onto the balcony, craning her neck to watch the rapidly expanding crowd milling around the Christmas tree in the small square at one end of the street.

'The local schools and churches organise it every year,' James explained, his lean hands resting a short space from hers on the parapet. 'Do you want to go down and join them while I mind Timmy?'

Not without you! She just about managed to bite back the words that sprang without warning to her lips, and, infinitely grateful for the darkness that concealed her wash of colour, shook her head.

'"In the Bleak Midwinter",' James murmured in recognition as the band and voices struck up again. 'I think it's one of my favourites.'

'Mine too,' Beth returned. They exchanged swift, conspiratorial grins and, no longer able to resist, added their voices to the rising swell below, the words of the carol having been committed to memory during childhood and never forgotten.

'Caroline's going to miss Timmy's first Christmas,' Beth mused in the ensuing lull, her eyes darkening with a rush of sympathy for James's sister—torn between her husband and child.

James nodded. 'I suppose you're going to spend Christmas Day with your aunt?' he asked idly.

Beth's hands tightened over the parapet. 'You mean I'm actually going to be given a twenty-four-hour pass?' she enquired dryly, neatly dodging a direct reply.

'At a pinch Timmy and I might just be able to spare you for Boxing Day too,' James conceded gravely. 'But no longer.'

He's only teasing you, Beth warned herself, trying to ignore the immediate glow his words had produced. He and Timmy would manage perfectly well without her. Then she forgot everything, the hairs standing up on the back of her neck as the silence was broken by the clear, pure voice of a lone choirboy.

As the last note died away, she swallowed hard and turned to James with a slightly self-conscious smile— her smile stiffening as she saw the direction of his gaze, the expression in the dark blue eyes focused intently on the wide curve of her mouth.

She'd barely registered the expression before it was gone, blue shutters slamming down over the dark-lashed eyes, making her wonder later if she'd imagined it. But in that fleeting second she'd never been so aware of James Fenner, not as her employer, not as Timmy's uncle, but simply as a man. A man who threatened not just her occasional peace of mind but her entire existence.

'It's getting cold,' he said abruptly. 'Shall we go in?'

She nodded, all her heightened senses alive to the formidable masculine presence beside her as she stepped through into the lounge. Silently she stood watching him fasten the windows, eyes moving edgily over the rigid back, wishing with all her heart that she could recapture that earlier mood of relaxed well-being.

As James turned round, she jerked her eyes away from him and swiftly walked over to the sofa, picked up the tray from the low table and headed for the door.

'I'd better go and make up Timmy's bottle for his late-night feed.'

She took a deep, calming breath as she entered the kitchen and started on her task. Sensing James's presence immediately, she glanced over her shoulder and saw him looming in the doorway, a sports bag clasped in his hand.

'I'm going down to the gym.'

'At this time of night?' she blurted out incredulously.

'It should be pretty quiet down there now.' He shrugged a muscular shoulder and turned away.

Was this part of his regular routine? Beth wondered in disbelief as she heard the front door close. Although he was undoubtedly fit, somehow she'd never visualised James Fenner as a dedicated fanatic.

Curiously Beth peeped through the glass door into the small but well-equipped air-conditioned room beyond. If the gym had been quiet when James had visited it last night, this afternoon it was totally deserted.

Readjusting the bag slung over her shoulder, she took hold of the pushchair again and wheeled it on down the empty corridor into the equally empty changing rooms.

'Looks like we're going to have the pool to ourselves,' Beth murmured to her tiny companion, depositing her bag on a bench.

Until his departure to Stanton Enterprises just before lunch, she'd spent the bulk of the morning working with James in his office. Not that she'd achieved a great deal during those hours, she admitted ruefully. She'd found it difficult to concentrate, her mind wandering off at uncomfortable tangents. Fortunately James had seemed equally preoccupied, and had made no comment on her limited output. Neither, to her surprise, had he left her a list of instructions to be carried out during his absence.

'So while the cat's away, hmm, Tim?'

Selecting a locker, Beth stripped off her clothes, pulled on her black swimsuit and turned her attention to Timmy.

'All set?' she enquired with a grin a few minutes later as she looked down at the tiny figure in her arms, swathed in his bright orange inflatable armbands. 'Colour suits you,' she assured him, and, wary of slipping on the tiled floor, strapped him back in his pushchair and wheeled him out to the poolside.

She came to an abrupt halt. She'd been wrong. The pool wasn't empty—an instantly recognisable male form was cutting through the water with effortless ease.

What on earth was he doing here when right now he ought to be several miles away in his office? Transfixed, Beth watched as he executed a deft tumble-turn and came powering back towards her. Reaching the shallow end, his long legs floated under him and he stood upright.

'I saw your note when I came in,' he drawled casually. 'You must have only just left the flat when I arrived.'

Beth barely heard him, her breath lodging in her throat, caught completely unprepared for the effect of that gleaming, naked male torso.

Droplets of water trickled off the wide, powerful shoulders, glistened on the matt of fine dark hair that covered the strong chest and trailed a shadowy path over the flat stomach before disappearing beneath the waterline.

Oh, God, she was standing there gawping at him like an adolescent! Then came the equally disturbing realisation that James was appraising her with the same degree of thoroughness, the blue eyes sweeping over her slender curves with undisguised male interest.

With horror she felt her whole body tauten, responding to the blatant masculine gaze as if it had been a physical caress, the knowing blue gleam assuring her that her reaction hadn't passed unnoticed.

Battling to maintain an outward composure, determinedly ignoring the warmth gushing through her, Beth unstrapped Timmy unhurriedly and carried him carefully to the water's edge. Passing him into James's outstretched arms, she slipped thankfully into the pool.

Fully supported by his buoyant suit, Timmy bobbed up and down, gurgling with delight as he enthusiastically splashed the water with his tiny arms. It was impossible not to be affected by his innocent happiness, impossible not to return James's amused smile.

'Go and have a swim,' he instructed her lazily,

keeping a vigilant eye and steadying hand on his tiny nephew.

She obeyed without demur, lapping the pool several times with a leisurely front crawl before rejoining them. Then she took charge of Timmy while James swam.

She'd always considered herself a competent swimmer but she wasn't in James's league, Beth admitted, half watching him over Timmy's head. Of course he did have a decided advantage with his long, lean legs and wide, powerful shoulders. Her mouth went dry. A perfect swimmer's physique.

'I think Tim's had enough,' she greeted James as he returned to her side, his hair plastered to his head like a sleek, dark pelt.

She wondered whether he'd elect to remain in the pool, but, after assisting her out of the water with Timmy, he headed for the changing room. And when she emerged some time later from the adjoining one she discovered him waiting for her with no sign of impatience by the lift at the end of the corridor.

'What time are you going out tonight?' he enquired, transferring his sports bag from his hand to his shoulder as he helped her into the lift with Timmy.

Beth jolted, realising with a surge of guilt that until James's reminder she'd forgotten all about her date with David Richardson.

'Sevenish,' she answered vaguely as the lift began its ascent. She would have to allow herself sufficient time to cross to the other side of the city. It would have made more sense to have arranged a venue nearer James's flat, she supposed, but that would have necessitated explanations she didn't feel inclined to make. Besides, she could use the opportunity to check on her own flat and collect any mail.

'Does David have a car?'

'Not as far as I know.' What was all this? Beth shot him an upward glance.

'Don't come back on your own on the underground,' he said quietly. 'Get a taxi, hmm?'

Beth nodded, her chest suddenly tightening. She couldn't remember the last time anyone had actually worried about her. The fact that his concern was groundless, that she'd fully intended to get a taxi anyway, was neither here nor there. Her growing suspicion that James was by nature highly protective of anyone smaller and weaker than himself—regardless of who they were—wasn't important either.

The tiny little glow remained with her later as she fed and prepared Timmy for bed and then took him to say goodnight to James, who'd disappeared into his office almost immediately they'd entered the flat.

She tapped on his door and, when he didn't respond, assumed that he was probably too engrossed to have heard, and walked in.

Arms folded behind his head, he was leaning back in his chair, feet propped up on his empty desk, dark, unreadable eyes focused on the wall opposite.

'James?'

'Mmm?' He turned his head, frowning as if still lost in thought, and then abruptly jerked himself to his feet. 'Is it Timmy's bedtime already?' Absently he retrieved the sports bag he'd discarded casually by his desk and slung it over his shoulder. 'I didn't realise it was so late.'

Amazing how quickly time flies when you're

busy... Beth suppressed her grin as he crossed the room.

'Goodnight, Tim, old chap.'

Timmy's thumb stole into his mouth, his eyelids flickering downwards. Beth's arms tightened around him. 'He almost fell asleep over his bottle,' she said softly.

'Infants have no stamina these days,' James said sadly, accompanying her into the hall.

Beth grinned, her eyes alighting by chance on the embossed initials on his sports bag.

'What does "B" stand for?' she asked suddenly, unable to conceal her curiosity any longer.

He looked puzzled for a second and then, following her gaze, his eyes cleared. 'Bach,' he said solemnly.

'Bark?' Beth repeated dubiously, searching his face unsuccessfully to discover whether she was being teased again. 'As in dog?'

The corners of the straight mouth twitched. 'As in my father's favourite composer. Fortunately,' he continued, his grin broadening, 'by the time Sarah was born, my parents had come to their senses.'

Beth gave a muffled snort of laughter. She didn't want to go out with David tonight—didn't want to be anywhere but here with James. Would it be terribly mean to phone David and cancel their date at this late stage? It wasn't as if their relationship was anything more than a casual friendship. He probably wouldn't mind. The buzz of the outer door cut through her indecisive thoughts.

'That'll probably be Julia,' James murmured, glancing at his wristwatch as he moved towards the intercom on the wall.

Beth didn't wait for confirmation; she turned and headed swiftly towards Timmy's bedroom. What a prize idiot she was. Hadn't it occurred to her that James might actually welcome her absence from the flat for the evening? Appreciate a few hours' privacy in his own home?

'More coffee?'

'No, thanks.' Beth smiled at the fair-headed man sitting opposite her across the red and white checked tablecloth. She felt relaxed and pleasantly soporific, had enjoyed the evening in David's cheerful, uncomplicated company far more than she'd anticipated.

'Shall we make a move?' he suggested, returning her smile.

She nodded. 'Otherwise I'm going to fall asleep!'

'My conversation's that stimulating?' He grinned, turning his head to catch the waiter's attention.

Beth grinned back. It was impossible not to like David Richardson. He was easygoing and comfortable to be with. Unlike James. Oh, damn! She'd vowed not to think about James, had been determined not to dwell on that expression of polite indifference on his face when she'd popped her head around the lounge door to announce her departure. He'd been sitting on the sofa beside Julia... Resolutely she turned her attention back to David.

After splitting the bill at Beth's insistence, they collected their coats and emerged from the warmth of the cheerful, family-run pub restaurant into the chill of the night air.

'I'll walk you back to your flat,' David murmured,

reaching casually for her hand as they headed along the deserted street.

'Thanks.' As she smiled up into his open, good-natured face, she felt a twinge of guilt at the subterfuge yet no real temptation to tell him of her temporary change of address. The pressure of his fingers against hers felt warm and companionable but no more than that, she registered. No tiny little frisson of excitement, no tingle of anticipation.

His brief goodnight kiss when they arrived outside the converted Victorian house where she lived was pleasant, but left her equally unmoved. Not knowing whether to be relieved or disappointed by her lack of response, Beth watched David walk down the front path, returning his goodbye wave as he reached the street, and closed the front door.

Thoughtfully she made her way up the communal staircase to her flat on the first floor. As much as she liked him, she was suddenly certain that she didn't want her relationship with David to progress any further than its present, basically platonic friendship.

Unlocking the door of her flat, she picked up her accumulated mail and flicked through it. Two Christmas cards from old schoolfriends and a pile of circulars. Depositing them on the hall table, she made a swift inspection of the flat then returned to the hall to phone for a taxi.

After replacing the receiver, she went into the small living room to wait, immediately conscious of the engulfing, unbroken silence as she sat down on the elderly but comfortable sofa. As her eyes wandered round the room that she had painstakingly decorated and furnished over the last year, she wondered why it suddenly seemed so sterile and empty.

She frowned. She loved her small, cosy flat, was proud of the work she'd put into it. She liked living on her own, treasured the solitude. So why did she suddenly feel so appallingly lonely?

With relief she heard the buzz of the doorbell and, checking first to ensure that it was the taxi, carefully locked up the flat then, clutching her handbag, made her way swiftly back down the stairs.

It was rather like an action replay, she mused some time later as the taxi discharged her outside James's block of flats. Except that tonight everything seemed completely familiar. Entering the building, she crossed the foyer to the lift with assured footsteps, aware of the teasing little tingle beginning to creep down her spine.

Would he still be up? Shaking her head ruefully, she stepped out of the lift. She'd been kissed tonight by an extremely good-looking, personable young man and felt absolutely nothing. And yet her pulse rate had suddenly doubled just at the thought of getting a brief glimpse of James before she went to bed!

Her eyes troubled, she paused outside the door of the flat. It wasn't the thought of living in James's home for another few weeks that had thrown her into such a panic yesterday, she admitted with painful honesty, but the thought of leaving it at the end of that time. And the longer she stayed here, the harder it was going to be to return to her strictly office-based working relationship with James.

Slowly she inserted the key in the door and pushed it open, closing it quietly behind her. The hall light had been left on, but the lounge and kitchen lay in darkness. So he'd already gone to bed. As she hung up her coat, she was conscious of the scent of perfume, a lingering reminder of Julia's earlier presence.

She stiffened abruptly, her stomach cramping in a fierce knot. What a naive little fool she was sometimes. Why hadn't it dawned on her that Julia might very well still be here in the flat?

Silently Beth made her way down the hall, keeping her eyes focused rigidly ahead as she passed James's bedroom door. She paused briefly to check on Timmy and then sped on swiftly to her own room.

After preparing mechanically for bed, she slipped under the duvet and switched off the bedside light. Hands clenching painfully by her sides, she stared bleakly up into the darkness.

CHAPTER SIX

'OH, TIMMY, darling, what's the matter?' Beth asked beseechingly, gazing down with concern at the flushed, screwed-up little face in her arms as she paced up and down the room. Muffling a yawn, she flicked a quick glance at her wristwatch. One-thirty in the morning. It felt a lot later. Contrary to her expectation, she must have fallen asleep the moment her head hit the pillow; Timmy's cries of distress had roused her from a dreamless slumber.

'Surely you can't be hungry again already?' she queried uncertainly. It was possible, she supposed, that James, distracted by Julia, might have forgotten to give Timmy his late feed. But somehow she doubted it.

As soon as Timmy had calmed down a bit she would go and make up a bottle anyway, Beth decided, turning round as she reached the window and walking back across the carpet. To her relief Timmy's heart-wrenching sobs gradually subsided, his eyelashes beginning to flicker downwards as he sucked feverishly on his thumb. Laying him gently down in his cot, she started for the door, but before she'd reached it he began to cry again.

Defeatedly she scooped him up into her arms once more, and looked up, instantly aware of James's presence.

Clad in a white towelling robe, his hair ruffled, he towered in the doorway.

'What's up, then, Tim?' he murmured softly, the robe gaping over his broad chest as he crossed the carpet.

Didn't he possess any pyjamas? Beth wondered irritably, her stomach lurching as she unsuccessfully tried to ignore the expanse of firm, male skin.

'There was no need for you to get up. I can manage perfectly well.' She was aware of how cold and ungracious she sounded, but just wanted him gone from the room. Weakened by tiredness, she felt too vulnerable and defenceless to arm herself safely against that all-pervading maleness.

'Have you given him some syrup?' he enquired shortly, a muscle flickering along the line of his shadowy jaw. His eyes narrowed as she frowned uncomprehendingly. 'Paracetamol syrup,' he elaborated curtly. 'He's probably teething.'

She groaned inwardly. Of course. How could she have been so dense as to not have worked that out for herself? She suddenly felt totally inadequate, useless. James should have employed a professional nanny, she thought miserably. It would have been much fairer on Timmy.

'There's a bottle of it and a spoon in the kitchen cupboard where his food is,' James added brusquely. In the dim lighting, his eyes were dark blue, fathomless pools.

'I'll fetch it,' Beth said tightly as he made no move to do so. He didn't have to sound accusatory. She'd warned him she knew next to nothing about babies, and she hadn't had the advantage of a crash-course from his sister. She could see the strong pulse beating at the base of his neck, her sense of smell overwhelmed by the minty freshness of his breath and the clean, soapy scent of his skin as he reached to take hold of Timmy. Her stomach muscles knotting, she turned swiftly towards the door.

'And go and put on a damn dressing gown as well.'

Startled, Beth shot him a frigid glare over her shoulder. How dared he sound so censorious? Her full-length, high-necked nightdress, presented to her last Christmas by her aunt and worn for the first time tonight, was the epitome of propriety, and far more decent than his revealing bathrobe.

'Oh, for God's sake, Beth,' he growled. 'With the light behind you, that thing is virtually transparent.'

What? Mortified, she turned away and fled to her room, her eyes shooting instinctively to the full-length mirror opposite her as she stood momentarily illuminated in the doorway. Transparent, my foot! she thought. All that could be seen through the white cotton—and that was on the closest scrutiny—was a faint, shadowy silhouette, just the barest hint of slender curves. Hardly cause for James to sound like some outraged Victorian papa. Especially as she was damn sure he'd seen women in far skimpier lingerie.

Grabbing her robe, she tied it securely around her slim body and started back towards the kitchen, tensing as she saw James's open bedroom door. How could she walk by and not even glance in? She couldn't, she admitted weakly as her eyes darted to the right.

A green and white duvet lay tossed to one side on the empty king-sized bed. Beth expelled a deep breath of air as she hurried into the kitchen. So she wouldn't have to make polite conversation with Julia over the breakfast table after all.

She discovered the bottle of infant syrup stowed away at the back of the cupboard behind a pile of tins. Couldn't James have put it somewhere a little more prominent so that she might have seen it earlier? she wondered tetchily as she returned to Timmy's room.

James was standing with his back to her, the white towelling robe taut across the width of his powerful shoulders. His calves were muscular, and liberally sprinkled with fine dark hairs. She swallowed hard, avoiding his eyes as he turned round.

Timmy was sound asleep in his arms. Raising his dark eyebrows wryly, James gently placed him in his cot. Timmy's eyes remained firmly closed.

'Goodnight.' Not waiting for a reply, Beth swung round and headed down the hall to her room. She resisted the temptation to glance back over her shoulder until she reached her door, and was just in time to see James disappearing not into his bedroom but in the direction of his office. Surely he wasn't going to start working now? The man was certifiable. Well, as long as he didn't expect her to join him. She closed her bedroom door.

'Read that last paragraph back to me, please, Beth,' James requested imperiously, leaning back in his chair.

Sighing under her breath, she flipped over the pages of her notebook and began to translate her shorthand out loud.

'Wake up, Beth,' he cut in tersely. 'That last sentence is a figment of your imagination. It doesn't even make sense; it's completely out of context.'

She gritted her teeth and deleted the offending sentence. It hadn't made sense when he'd first dictated it, but he'd overruled her tentative enquiry at the time. She looked at him balefully from under her lashes, noting the lines of weariness etched into his face.

Had he slept at all last night? He'd already been ensconced in his office by the time she and Timmy had appeared for breakfast that morning, so whether he'd merely showered and dressed after working all through the night, or had actually gone to bed, she had no way of knowing.

What on earth had been so important that it couldn't have waited a few more hours anyway? She refused to feel any sympathy for him. He was like the proverbial bear with a sore head this morning, and she was the one in the firing line, taking the brunt of his foul mood.

Timmy, taking a short break from executive decision-making, was sitting on his play-mat on the carpet. Fortunately completely oblivious to the tension in the room, he was chuckling to himself as he vainly attempted to tug the ears off his toy white rabbit.

Beth's fingers gripped her pencil as James resumed dictation, his normal, fluid style today punctuated by long, uncharacteristic pauses. She flicked him a glance as he halted once again. He was dressed casually this morning in black jeans and a black shirt which, Beth thought gloomily, not only reflected his mood but presumably indicated that he was planning to work from home all day.

'Have you typed up the minutes from the board meeting yet?' he demanded as he completed his dictation.

She didn't even bother to answer. He knew perfectly well she hadn't. Or had he expected her to sit up all night working too?

'And the bulk of yesterday's mail still needs attention.' He indicated the pile of letters he'd placed in her tray earlier. 'Perhaps you could make a start on them first.'

Deciding it was safer to nod than speak, Beth dutifully began slicing open the envelopes, dividing the correspondence into two piles as normal—those letters she could deal with herself and those that required James's attention.

'I'd like to see a draft of every reply before you print a top copy.'

What? Sweeping her hair back over her shoulder, Beth looked at James in disbelief. This was getting utterly absurd. He was treating her like a junior copy-typist. A lot of the correspondence required standard replies, others merely requested confirmation of meetings, hotel bookings, travel itineraries—all of which she'd originally arranged anyway.

Lips compressed, she savagely ripped open the next envelope. James was a hard taskmaster, but he'd always been reasonably fair. And she'd always assumed that he appreciated the fact that she could use her own initiative and didn't require constant, time-consuming supervision. And now he was questioning her competence in dealing with the most basic correspondence.

Her eyes rested briefly on Timmy. Lying on his

back, he was watching the sunlight play across the white ceiling with absorption. He looked peaceful and content, Beth mused, envying him his tranquillity.

She switched on her computer and started on the letters James had dictated earlier, cursing under her breath as she transposed two sentences. She cursed again as instead of rectifying the error she deleted the whole paragraph. How was she supposed to concentrate with James prowling around the room like a caged panther? She felt edgy enough already without the feeling that he was about to pounce any minute.

Turning her head, she studied him warily from under her lashes as he paused by the window. He looked cold and remote, his mouth clamped in a hard, unyielding line, his eyes a chilling blue beneath the black, forbidding brows. It was impossible to believe that those harsh, unresponsive features could ever soften into a smile, reflect warmth and amusement. Impossible to believe that this man had sauntered good-humouredly around a park with her a couple of days ago, feeding ducks.

Beth's eyes moved slowly over his granite face. How could anyone change so dramatically from one day to the next? But then, she thought resignedly, James Fenner could alter from hour to hour. She frowned. He hadn't been quite so unpredictable when she'd first come to work for him, had he? It was only in the last few months, she reflected, that his mood swings had become so pronounced and erratic. Lost in thought, she was caught completely off guard as he spun round to face her.

'I don't pay you to sit and daydream,' he rasped, and strode back to his desk.

Stony-faced, Beth focused her eyes on the screen in front of her, her fingers moving mechanically over the keyboard. Feel angry, feel resentful, feel hard done by—but for Pete's sake don't feel hurt, she ordered herself.

But she would have needed an anaesthetic not to be aware of the stab of pain at his curt reminder that her role in his flat and in his life was strictly that of paid employee and nothing more. He evidently regretted the increasing familiarity that had been creeping into their relationship over the past few days and was determined to put it back on a strictly professional basis.

She jerked her eyes to the dark head. 'I assume that next month's salary will reflect my increased working hours?' she enquired, and to her satisfaction saw the blue eyes narrow slightly at her cold, mercenary tone.

'Naturally,' he answered shortly.

Exchanging scowls with him, Beth turned back to her tasks. So that was that. The status quo had been firmly resumed, the barriers between them securely back in place.

At the stroke of twelve Beth switched off her screen and placed the dust-cover over the top. Gathering up those letters she'd completed, she carried them across the room and placed them unceremoniously in front of James.

'You haven't finished them all,' he said tersely, flipping through the pile.

'No,' she agreed. 'I haven't.' And as far as she was concerned they could wait until Monday or even until after Christmas, because she had absolutely no inten-

tion of spending any more of the weekend cooped up
with James in his office.

'It's time for Timmy's lunch,' she said evenly.
'And this afternoon I'm taking him for a walk.' She
paused. 'I assume Timmy takes precedence over routine mail?' she finished sweetly.

The blue eyes were expressionless. 'If you utilised
your time more effectively, there wouldn't be a con-
flict,' he said coolly. His gaze dropped back dismissively to the open file in front of him.

Beth stood motionless for a second, her eyes resting
speculatively on the bowed dark head. How had he
survived this long with just a broken nose? If his
moods were erratic, hers were equally so—because
right now she wished with all her heart that she could
walk out of this flat and never lay eyes on James
Fenner again.

She crossed the carpet and picked up Timmy,
glancing swiftly back over her shoulder at the silent,
seated figure as she reached the door. And in that
fleeting second she caught him off guard, witnessed a
mirror image of her own expression on the dark face.
He was as relieved by her departure from the room
as she was by her escape.

'If your uncle finds my presence in his home so irk-
some, why did he ask me there in the first place?'
Beth muttered. Her hands gripped firmly around the
pushchair, she overtook two teenaged girls as she cir-
cuited the small park for the second time.

'And, instead of just getting in a foul mood, why
doesn't he admit he's made a mistake, admit that he
hadn't realised what a strain it would be living under

the same roof as me?' She was under a similar strain and she wasn't snappy and bad-tempered, she thought bitterly.

'And if that's the way he feels, why did he ask me to stay on until your mummy gets back?' she demanded, and, oblivious to the curious stare of a passing jogger, gave an inelegant snort. 'I use the term "ask" in the widest sense.'

Timmy beamed up at her.

'You're not taking this seriously!' she admonished him.

He waved his small mittened hands in the air apologetically.

'OK, you're forgiven.' Beth's mouth curved as she looked down at him, resisting the urge to pick him up and hug him. There were definite compensations in this present situation. She took a deep, calming breath, drinking in the crisp afternoon air, her strides shortening as she slowed her pace. 'And the topic of James Fenner is now firmly closed.' She wasn't going to mention his name again or even think about him—for at least five minutes.

Her grin widened. Was she imagining that expression of relief in Timmy's large blue eyes? Dodging a determined-looking, small, duffle-coated figure astride a tricycle, she exchanged smiles with the child's apologetic mother and then glanced at her watch.

'Time we were heading back, Tim.' She stopped to tuck his rug back round him. 'If I can remember the way,' she added thoughtfully as she straightened up. She hadn't paid a great deal of attention to her surroundings on her outward journey, she admitted wryly; she had been too intent on getting as far away from James as quickly as possible.

She burst into laughter as Timmy fixed her with an unwavering, disapproving stare. She could visualise James's reaction to the same confession so clearly, could almost hear the deep, caustic voice.

Emerging from the park, she paused to get her bearings. 'Across the square, past the row of mews cottages and then first left,' she decided out loud as she propelled the pushchair forward, grateful that her subconscious mind had absorbed more than she'd realised.

A burst of adrenalin surged through her, her steadily increasing pace reflecting her quickening pulse rate as she retraced her earlier route. It wasn't until she turned into the familiar street that she recognised with disgusted disbelief that she was now hurrying back to James with the same sense of urgency with which she'd escaped him such a short time ago.

She sensed James's absence the second she opened the door of the flat, alerted not merely by the silence but by something far more intangible. Momentarily deflated, she hung up her coat, her disappointment changing swiftly to relief as she unstrapped a drowsy-eyed Timmy and picked him up. In her present keyed-up state it was probably a good thing that he wasn't here, she reflected. It would give her more time to get her see-sawing emotions back on an even keel.

Automatically, her gaze dropped to the hall table. James might be under no obligation to give her an account of his movements, but it would have been courteous to have left a note giving her some idea of when he expected to return.

Her eyes softened as she looked down at Timmy, planting a kiss on the top of his golden head as she carried him through to his room. He fell asleep in her arms before she'd removed his outer clothes, and didn't stir as the doorbell rang.

'All right, I'm coming,' Beth muttered under her breath, carefully laying Timmy in his cot before darting back into the hall to press the intercom.

'Yes?'

'Open the door, please, Beth,' commanded a deep, disembodied voice.

Beth studied the intercom thoughtfully. 'Why don't you use your key?' she suggested helpfully. 'Sorry, James, I didn't quite catch that.' Her eyes dancing, she released the outer door. Tut-tut, James. He *was* becoming absent-minded—forgetting business meetings, door keys...

Turning away, she sped back down the hall to her bedroom, dragged off her thick blue woollen jumper and replaced it with a long-sleeved olive and cream checked shirt, tucking it into the waistband of her jeans. She brushed her hair quickly, sweeping it back over her shoulders, and applied a faint sheen of lip gloss.

'No, I'm not doing this for James,' she assured the girl in the mirror. 'I'm doing it for me.'

The wide hazel eyes evinced doubts about her veracity.

'Sorry—haven't time to argue about it now,' Beth apologised as the doorbell pealed for the second time. Schooling her features into an impassive mask, she made her way to the front door and flung it open.

'For God's sake, Beth, always use the safety chain

when you're on your own,' growled a huge Christmas tree.

Before she had time to gather her wits, let alone think of a retort, the tree advanced towards her on jean-clad legs.

'Could you grab hold of this, please?' A long arm snaked out through the branches.

Bemused, Beth took hold of the proffered carrier bag, the name of an exclusive department store emblazoned on the front.

'Where's Tim?' Setting the tree down on the stand affixed to its base, James shrugged off his leather jacket, tossing it casually onto a peg, and folded back the sleeves of his shirt.

'Having a nap,' Beth said weakly. Where exactly had he managed to find a tree that size, and more to the point how on earth had he managed to bring it back to the flat unaided?

'Good.' James nodded approvingly. 'With any luck, I'll have this set up for him by the time he wakes up.' He hoisted the tree up, balancing it against a powerful shoulder, and strode on down the hall, dodging the overhead light-fittings with dexterity, and disappeared into the lounge.

'Beth...' There was an abrupt silence broken by a muffled curse, followed a few moments later by an off-key rendition of 'Jingle Bells'. 'Beth...'

'Coming...' Her eyes alight with laughter, the carrier bag clutched in her hand, Beth obeyed the summons.

James was standing in the centre of the room as she walked in, arms folded across his broad chest, surveying the Christmas tree in front of the French windows with satisfaction.

Turning his head, he raised a quizzical eyebrow.

'It's blocking the balcony,' Beth pointed out. 'And the light.' She frowned slightly, not quite trusting that glint in his eyes. Well, he had invited her opinion, hadn't he? 'Wouldn't it be better in that empty corner…?' The rat! The corner to the right of the fireplace hadn't been empty this morning; it had contained a small bookcase and a standard lamp. He'd rearranged the furniture deliberately, had been intending to put the tree there all along.

'Very funny.' She gave him a bored, 'children will be children' look, which should have squashed him at ten paces but only served to deepen the amusement in those brilliant blue eyes.

She held out for two seconds, but couldn't keep her face straight any longer, and grinned at him as he swiftly and easily repositioned the tree.

'Lights!' he ordered, clicking his fingers.

'Lights,' Beth echoed obediently, producing the boxed fairy lights from the carrier bag. She stood watching for a moment as he began to arrange them over the tree and then, extracting two large flat boxes from the carrier, placed them on a coffee-table and knelt down beside it. She opened the first box and smiled with pleasure at the array of silver baubles and delicately crafted miniature decorations—a trumpet, candlesticks, Father Christmas astride his reindeer-drawn sleigh, a drummer boy, angels.

Turning her attention to the second box, she lifted the lid and blinked. Bright, shiny baubles, nestling against rainbow-hued strands of glistening tinsel, winked up at her in a dazzling kaleidoscope of colour. With a snort of laughter, she extracted one of the novelties. A plastic Father Christmas, a manic beam on his face, crouched over a motorbike, with a stunned-looking reindeer riding pillion.

'Thought it'd appeal to Timmy,' James said loftily, sitting down on the sofa opposite her.

Beth gave him a severe look.

'OK.' He raised his hands defensively. 'I couldn't resist it.' He surveyed the two boxes with their vastly contrasting contents solemnly. 'Shall we take a vote?'

'Subtle or over the top?' Beth pondered gravely, following his gaze. 'Of course this is solely for Timmy's benefit...'

'He likes bright colours,' James stated knowledgeably, and paused. 'We could always compromise...'

'Put the whole lot on...'

'Motion carried unanimously.' Unfolding his long frame from the sofa, James rose to his full height and extended a lean hand towards Beth.

Hesitating only for a second, she took hold of it and scrambled to her feet, instantly aware of the warmth shooting down her arm, the bubble of happiness welling up inside her. Stay on an even keel, she warned herself, conscious of just how fragile that bubble was, and how quickly it could burst.

'If you'd like to decorate the lower branches,' he instructed, 'I'll see to the higher ones.'

'Yes, James,' Beth said meekly, hiding her grin as she selected a silver bauble. Regardless of the situation, he just couldn't help taking command, issuing orders, could he? Hanging the decoration on the tree, she watched him from under her lashes as he stretched up a long, muscular arm to drape a piece of tinsel across a branch.

Pensively she inspected the two boxes of decorations. The candlesticks? Or would they look better on one of the higher branches? Perhaps one of the brighter baubles would be better next. Red or green?

'For heaven's sake, Beth, we are running on a very tight schedule. If you're going to spend five minutes deliberating over every single decoration...'

Beth jerked her head up as she heard the familiar exasperation in the deep voice. He just couldn't be pleasant to her for more than two minutes, could he? He just had to start criticising, start sniping at her. And she'd innocently thought this was supposed to be fun!

'This isn't a time and motion study,' she flared, and cursed inwardly as, too late, she absorbed the expression in the vivid blue eyes.

'Why do you do it?' she demanded abruptly. 'Why do you deliberately bait me, wind me up all the time?' And why did she always seem to lose her sense of humour where he was concerned, become over-sensitive and touchy?

'Do I?' he drawled idly, the blue eyes moving thoughtfully over her flushed face.

'You know perfectly well you do.'

'I can't resist it,' he finally conceded, the straight mouth quirking.

'Try!' Beth retorted acidly. Did it amuse him to provoke her then sit back and watch her getting steamed up about nothing? He'd probably done exactly the same thing to his sisters when he was a boy.

'You're very teasable, Beth.'

'At least I haven't got a warped sense of humour...'

'You look beautiful when you're angry.'

'Well, you don't,' she assured him, and, picking up a bauble, tossed it at him. He caught it deftly in his right hand and transferred it to the tree.

She wasn't one of his sisters, and she wasn't his whipping boy when he was in a bad mood. Selecting her next missile, Beth threw it at his head. He fielded it with the same dexterity as before and hung it on a branch.

'Keep them coming,' he ordered calmly over his broad shoulder.

It wasn't quite the leisurely, companionable way she'd envisaged decorating the tree, but it was certainly efficient, Beth mused dryly as she lobbed a succession of baubles across the room. As James attached the last one to the tree, she studied the laden branches.

'Needs more tinsel,' she decided firmly, fishing out a handful of purple and cerise strands from the box. Crossing the room, she draped the tinsel over the branches.

'That clashes,' James observed thoughtfully from behind her.

'I know,' Beth agreed with satisfaction, taking a step backwards to admire her handiwork. Her eyes moved up the tree, following the slender trunk to where it just grazed the high ceiling. 'Just the silver star to go on at the top.' Picking it up from the coffee-table, Beth held it out expectantly to James.

'Can't reach.' He smiled down at her blandly. 'You've pine needles in your hair.'

'Use one of the kitchen stools.'

'No head for heights,' he said sadly. Casually he stretched out a hand.

'That must have been somewhat of a handicap when you were climbing mountains,' Beth said caustically, trying to block her mind to her tingling scalp as his fingers brushed through her hair. 'Right, I'll do it myself.'

'Fair enough,' he agreed. 'How's your shoulder?'

'My shoulder?' She frowned, taken aback by the sudden change of conversation. 'Much better.'

'Good.'

She was caught completely off guard as his hands snaked around her waist and swung her up in the air. For a brief second her face was on a level with his and then, as effortlessly as if she'd been Timmy, he lifted her above his head, his arms folding around her hips.

'This isn't funny,' she muttered, one hand clutching the silver star, the other clamped to his shoulder as he moved into position by the Christmas tree. Not the least bit funny, she thought savagely. Keep a grip, Beth, she told herself. How was she supposed to do that with James's arms around her, the length of her body resting against unyielding male muscle...? She could feel the rise and fall of his hard chest, the rhythm of her own breathing beginning to match his.

'Can you reach?' James enquired solicitously, his head thrown back as he looked up at her.

It was the first time she'd ever had the height advantage over James, and it was disconcerting to see how much younger he looked from her rare vantage point. The hard contours of his face were softened. There was even the faintest suspicion of vulnerability at the back of the brilliant blue eyes, around the firm mouth... James Fenner vulnerable? Now that really was an illusion—a trick of the angle, the mellow light.

'Yes, I can reach,' she snarled at the dark head.

''Tis the season of peace and goodwill to all mankind,' James murmured benignly.

Beth ignored him, concentrating her whole effort on fastening the star to the tree as quickly as possible.

'It looks very effective off-centre like that,' the deep voice commented admiringly.

Ignoring him again, Beth repositioned the star. 'You can let me down now,' she ordered, her eyes dropping to his head.

James raised a dark eyebrow.

'Please,' she added witheringly.

He eased his hold, letting her slither to the ground in front of him, but didn't release her completely.

'Thank you,' she said sweetly as her feet touched the carpet, and looked pointedly at the hands resting lightly on her waist. She frowned, suddenly conscious of the protracted silence, the thoughtful expression in the blue eyes as they moved over her face and dropped with great deliberation to the curve of her mouth. More games? Refusing to let him ruffle her, she looked up at him disdainfully. She didn't believe for one moment that he had any intention of carrying out the wordless threat; he was just bluffing, trying to rattle her...

'Happy Christmas,' the deep voice murmured dryly a second before the firm, hard mouth brushed her cheek.

'It's not Christmas for three days,' Beth muttered. Damn it, James Fenner, if you're going to kiss me, at least do it properly—not as if I were your maiden aunt, she seethed. For one awful moment she thought she'd actually voiced the words out loud and then, as she encountered his fully aware eyes, she realised that her expression must have betrayed her as forcefully as any words.

Did it give his fragile male ego a fillip to know that he could reduce her to a quivering wreck with no more than a peck on the cheek? she wondered bitterly. Mustering as much dignity as she could, she looked squarely up into his face.

'I'll go and see if Timmy's awake,' she said coolly.

'Happy New Year, Beth,' James drawled, lowering his head towards her. This time his mouth grazed her forehead.

'It's n-not New Year for over a week,' she mumbled weakly. Why was he doing this? she wondered desperately. Because it amused him? And why was she just standing there like a mindless lump of jelly?

She forced herself to look up at him, her stomach lurching as she met the intense, dark blue gaze that was devoid of all mockery, aware that his hand had dropped to her hips as he drew her unprotestingly towards him.

'Happy Birthday, Beth.' She could feel the warmth of his breath on her cheek as his other hand curved around the nape of her neck, tilting her face up towards him.

'It's n-not my birthday until Jan...' The words drowned in her throat, relief shuddering through her as the warm, firm mouth finally claimed hers. Her eyelids flickered downwards, the knowing, expert mouth seducing all rational, coherent thought, coaxing, teasing her until she ached with slow, sensuous pleasure. Dizzily she swayed against him, her arms locking around his neck as she began kissing him back.

In that moment something changed, pleasure exploding into driving need as his kiss deepened, the hard mouth no longer persuasive but demanding, moving with increasing urgency against her parted lips. The warmth curdling in the pit of her stomach ignited into flames, heat scorching through her veins, radiating to every nerve-ending in her body. Then, with an abruptness that nearly made her cry out in protest, he lifted his head, his hands dropping to his sides.

Disorientated, her breathing erratic, Beth searched his face with wide, dazed eyes.

'Timmy...' he muttered huskily, a muscle flickering along the side of his lean jaw.

For the first time Beth registered the tiny, summoning wail.

'I'd b-better go and ch-check on him.' If only she could break away from the mesmerising eyes that were holding her immobile. Summoning every ounce of will-power, Beth turned away, forcing her shaking legs to cross the carpet towards the door.

The moment she was out of vision she paused, taking a deep, steadying breath. Don't start analysing what happened, she warned herself as her pulse rate returned to something near normal. Don't start building skyscrapers on the foundation of one kiss.

'Who, me?' she enquired severely of the facing wall. 'What kiss?' She shrugged her slim shoulders dismissively, and then grinned idiotically. She didn't feel like being sensible and rational, didn't want to forget those moments in James's arms. She wanted to relive them over and over in her head, wallow in them. Adrenalin spurting through her in warm, tingling waves, she hurried on down the hall.

Peeping around Timmy's door, she saw him lying on his back, gazing up at the butterfly mobile above his cot. As she walked in, he turned his head, focusing sad, reproachful eyes on her face.

'Feeling lonesome?' she murmured softly, scooping him up in her arms. Nestling against her breast, he beamed at her shyly.

'Not going coy on me, Tim?' She grinned, and hugged him as she made her way back along the hall. She was going to miss him when Caroline returned, she mused—and faltered, her mood of exhilaration ebbing at the cold realisation that once that happened she would in all likelihood never see him again. She would never see him crawl, take his first, shaky steps, hear him lisp his first words. Never know him as a toddler, a small boy.

She looked down into the guileless blue eyes, confused by the sense of loss, the emptiness gnawing inside her, the sudden longing... Oh, surely she wasn't getting broody? She'd never considered herself overly maternal, and although she'd always expressed the right degree of admiration when her various college and school friends exhibited their tiny offspring she'd always secretly preferred that offspring when she or he reached the toddler stage.

Of course she'd always assumed that in the natural course of things she would one day fall in love, get married and have children—those children a much wanted consequence of that love. But it had always been some time in the shadowy future. Not yet.

Her eyes veiled over. She'd also naively assumed that when she did fall in love she would be loved in return. She pulled herself up sharply, but it was too late—the warm glow inside her had been completely extinguished. At least, she supposed resignedly, it would be easier facing James again now her feet were firmly back on the ground.

She was about to walk into the lounge when she heard the faint rumble of his voice from behind the closed door, followed a few seconds later by the ting of the telephone receiver being replaced. So he'd taken advantage of her absence to make a private call. To Julia? Her muscles cramped at the confirmation—not that she'd really needed it—of just how meaningless and instantly forgettable their shared kiss had been to him.

Blanking her expression, she pushed open the lounge door and came to an immediate standstill, everything momentarily forgotten at the sight of the shimmering Christmas tree, the fairy lights the only illumination in the darkened room.

Instinctively she glanced down at Timmy to see his reaction, and her lips curved. What reaction? He was staring disapprovingly up at the shadowy ceiling as if suspecting it of harbouring cobwebs.

'Look at the tree, Tim,' she murmured encouragingly, conscious of James's silent approach across the carpet. Obligingly Timmy focused his eyes briefly in the direction she'd requested and then, evidently deciding she'd been sufficiently humoured, returned to his ceiling inspection.

'Once you've seen one Christmas tree, you've seen them all.' Laughing softly, Beth raised her head and, unable to put it off any longer, looked directly at James for the first time since she'd entered the room, her composure immediately dented as he gave her a slow, lazy smile.

'Blasé at six months?' He lifted a dark eyebrow as he stretched up a lean hand and switched on the wall lights.

At the sound of his uncle's voice, Timmy immediately turned his head, and with a delighted smile began flapping his arms towards him.

'I'll take him, shall I?' James drawled.

Not deceived for a second by the airy nonchalance in his voice, Beth placed Timmy in the strong, waiting arms, flicking a glance upwards into the dark face, her heart constricting at the gentleness tempering the carved male features.

Unobserved, her eyes moved over the square, tenacious jaw, and dropped to the decisive mouth. She swallowed. How was she ever going to be able to look at him again without remembering, without wanting...? She was practically drooling over him, she thought with self-disgust, averting her eyes swiftly.

'I'll go and make a start on Timmy's tea.' From now on, she thought resolutely, Timmy was going to be the only male uppermost in her thoughts.

'Give me a shout when it's ready.' James crossed to the sofa and sat down, balancing Timmy on his knees. 'I've asked Mrs Andrews to babysit tonight,' he added absently, almost as an afterthought.

En route to the door, Beth stopped. Ignore the bait, she ordered herself, but couldn't.

'Why?' Swinging around, she surveyed him suspiciously. She didn't trust that bland innocence on his face for one moment, couldn't believe that she was being given two nights off in a row.

'You think we should take Timmy with us?' He looked down into the small face thoughtfully. 'I'm not sure if his table manners are up to dining out yet. Or his teeth,' he added reflectively.

'And mine are?' Beth enquired slowly, her eyes narrowing. What was he playing at now?

'Dammit all, Beth, will you stop looking at me like that?' he suddenly rasped. 'Why do you always look for an ulterior motive in everything I do or say?'

'Because you usually have one,' she flung back.

'I'm inviting you to have dinner, not tumble into bed with me!'

'As I'm not in the habit of *tumbling into bed* with anyone, I never supposed you were,' Beth snapped, hoping fervently that he would assume that the furious colour washing over her face was attributable to indignation, and not to the disturbing mental picture his words had instantly conjured up in her head. Unable to meet his gaze, she glowered at a point above the dark head.

'I don't usually have this problem when I invite a woman out to dinner,' James grunted to Timmy, who was staring with round, fascinated eyes at the two empty decoration boxes on the coffee-table.

'You haven't invited me, you've just assumed I would go.' Perversely, the unconscious male arrogance didn't aggravate Beth as much as the knowledge that his words were undoubtedly true. 'And I'm not a woman, I'm your secretary.' Even before she

saw the leap of amusement on the dark face, she knew
how ridiculous that had sounded.

'And the two are a contradiction in terms?' He
laughed softly.

'You know perfectly well what I mean,' she
snapped.

'And you know perfectly well you're more than
just my secretary.'

Oh, sure. So what's the punchline? Beth mused acidly, and jolted, her immediate scepticism changing to
uncertainty as her eyes locked with his. Slowly she
searched the opaque blue shadows, tiny little goose-
bumps beginning to tingle down her stiffening spine.
He wasn't teasing her…

'So what am I, James?' she asked evenly, and
somewhere in the back of the navy blue pools saw a
hesitancy she would have thought inconceivable in
this man.

'I don't know,' he said quietly, his words almost
drowned by a loud, demanding wail.

CHAPTER SEVEN

'"I DON'T know,'" Beth growled at the bath taps as she lay back in the warm, scented water, a towel wrapped turban-style around her freshly washed hair. It wasn't exactly the most satisfactory of answers from a usually articulate man accustomed to making snap decisions every day of his life. If Timmy hadn't chosen that precise moment to make it vociferously clear that he was feeling both neglected and hungry, would James have elaborated? She might, Beth mused, have a few discreet words with Timmy about the importance of timing!

She suspected, however, that James—who had probably instantly regretted the admission of his ambiguous feelings for her—had been more than a little relieved by his nephew's intervention. He'd certainly shown no inclination to resume the fascinating conversation later on—not that there had been much opportunity, with Timmy to feed and put to bed, she admitted.

'Could you be ready by seven?' James had enquired casually as she'd emerged from Timmy's room, and, giving her no time to answer, let alone remind him pedantically that she hadn't even accepted his invitation, he had disappeared in the direction of his own room.

Stepping out of the bath, she dried herself swiftly and, clad in her robe, padded into her bedroom, her lips twisting wryly as she caught sight of her reflection in the mirror. The confusion in her wide, luminous eyes was a much surer indication of the turmoil inside her than the contrived outward flippancy.

Just don't think, she ordered herself as she sat down in front of the dressing table with her hair-drier. Don't even try and second-guess what's going on in James's head. Don't start wondering why he's not seeing Julia tonight. Easier said than done, she sighed as her thoughts continued to whirl in increasingly unproductive circles.

Switching off the drier a few minutes later, she stood up, her glossy hair swinging across her shoulders as she walked across to the wardrobe. At least deciding what to wear wasn't going to be too taxing considering the limited choice on offer! More than grateful for the last-minute impulse that had prompted her to bring it with her, Beth extracted the V-necked black silk jersey dress and slipped it over her head. She knew without vanity that the dress suited her, the simple, flattering style timeless. Several years old now, it was also reassuringly familiar, and right now reassurance was something of which she was badly in need.

Zipping up the back, she inspected herself in the mirror and her lips twitched. She looked decidedly sick, she observed kindly, her dark-fringed eyes enormous against her ivory skin. More to the point, she felt sick, her stomach churning as if she were on a rollercoaster.

A wave of panic crawled through her. The evening was going to be a total disaster! No work, no Timmy as a buffer. Just undiluted James Fenner. Far from dazzling him with her sparkling conversation, she was probably going to sit opposite him tongue-tied, like a gauche adolescent. Or, even worse, after a couple of glasses of wine she might start gazing at him with dreamy, all too revealing eyes. Her mouth began to curve. Maybe she was overdoing the cheerful optimism...

Picking up her handbag, she left her bedroom and made her way down the hall, pausing instinctively outside Timmy's room. About to enter, she saw the tall, shadowy figure bending over the cot and, averting her eyes, hurried on swiftly past the open door, shying away from the disturbing emotions that the sight of James and his tiny nephew always evoked.

'You look lovely,' Mrs Andrews greeted Beth warmly as she walked into the lounge. The large bar of chocolate and best-selling paperback lying on the sofa beside her indicated how she planned to spend the evening.

'Thank you,' Beth smiled, the words doing wonders for her flagging confidence. Her smile stiffened as James sauntered into the room, her throat constricting. She'd seen him in a dark suit countless times in the office, so why did the sight of him tonight unnerve her so completely? The tie nestling against his brilliant white shirt was the same deep blue as his eyes. He looked urbane, assured and overwhelmingly male, the expert tailoring doing little to minimise the width of his shoulders or the length of his lean legs.

'Ready?' he enquired casually.

She nodded. Oh, God, tongue-tied already! Swallowing hard, she just about managed to murmur an audible farewell to Mrs Andrews before turning towards the door, acutely conscious of James's towering presence behind her as she walked down the hall.

'Thank you,' she mumbled as he helped her on with her coat, her sense of smell teased by his male scent. Closing the door behind them, he shepherded her across the thickly carpeted corridor and into the waiting lift.

Reaching out a lean hand, he pressed the 'down' button. 'If you'd like to wait in the lobby, I'll bring the car round to the front.'

'Thank you, James,' she said, and her lips curved, her tension abruptly evaporating. It was going to take some getting used to, this role reversal. Normally she was the one scurrying around making life as comfortable as possible for him! Her grin broadened as he raised an enquiring dark eyebrow at her.

'Nothing,' she dismissed innocently.

He didn't look convinced. 'Beth...' he threatened ominously.

'It's just that normally you'd have flung your keys at me and asked—no, ordered *me* to fetch the car.' Just as he had on countless occasions at the office when he'd been in a tearing hurry to get to some meeting.

'Only if it were raining,' he denied, his mouth beginning to quirk. 'Am I that much of a tyrant to work for?'

'Impossible,' she said cheerfully. It was quite extraordinary that he had such a low turnover of staff!

'And am I equally impossible to live with?' he drawled.

This was getting a little dangerous even though he

was only teasing. 'Hell,' Beth retorted lightly, avoiding his eyes on the pretext of checking that her handbag was securely fastened.

'Right, out you get,' he instructed as the lift ground to a halt.

'Yes, James,' she said meekly, rather enjoying the novelty of playing the delicate, fragile female to his dominant, protective male. She stepped into the lobby and turned round to watch the lift descend to the underground car park. Perhaps tonight wasn't going to be such an ordeal after all, she mused, warmth spurting through her as she crossed to the entrance.

Trying not to look like an excited teenager going out on her first date, Beth stepped out into the winter's night as the familiar silver saloon drew up outside.

'Warm enough?' James asked as she settled back luxuriously in the wide, comfortable passenger seat, stretching out her slim legs in front of her.

'Mmm,' she murmured as the powerful car moved off silently. Warm and happy. Unobserved, her eyes moved over his shadowed profile. She loved the angle of his square chin, the clean-cut line of his jaw. She smiled. And most of all that tiny bump on his otherwise perfect, straight nose.

Turning her head, she looked out of the window. 'It's sleeting,' she said in surprise, watching the windscreen-wipers disperse the transparent flakes of melting ice.

'It's been sleeting for the last five minutes,' James murmured dryly, and, stretching out a lean hand, switched on the radio.

Beth watched a taxi on the other side of the street discharge its passengers onto the pavement as she absently listened to the tail-end of the weather forecast. Blizzards in Scotland…parts of Yorkshire completely cut off…many roads impassable…more heavy snow-falls expected overnight…conditions worsening… spreading south…

She jolted. How long had half the country been under snow? she wondered in amazement, and real-ised that for the last few days she hadn't listened to the news on the radio or television, hadn't done so much as glance at the headlines of a newspaper. It wasn't because of lack of opportunity—she'd simply become increasingly insular, she realised with shock. Her world was beginning to revolve entirely around Timmy…and James.

'It might be a good idea if you travelled down to Wiltshire in the morning instead of waiting until Monday,' James said quietly.

Beth cursed silently. She was going to have to come clean before this situation became too compli-cated.

'Actually I'm not spending Christmas with my aunt this year,' she said casually. 'I'm staying in London.'

'I see. And when did you suddenly make this de-cision?'

She hadn't made the decision, it had been made for her, Beth thought wryly, deciding that she must have imagined the chilly disapproval in his voice.

'Yesterday evening?'

Beth's eyes jumped to James's face. What had yes-terday evening to do with it? And she most definitely hadn't imagined the coldness in his voice this time.

'You haven't visited your aunt once this year. And now you can't even put yourself out to spend

Christmas Day with her,' he said contemptuously.
'Have you even bothered to tell her of your last-
minute change of plan yet? Told her you've had a
better offer from your boyfriend?'

Her boyfriend? Everything suddenly clicked into
place in Beth's head. James thought that David had
asked her to spend Christmas with him last night and
that she had accepted, callously proposing to let her
aunt down at the last minute. If she hadn't felt so
angry she would have burst into laughter.

'How or with whom I spend Christmas is none of
your damn business,' she flared. 'And it's Aunt Mary
who doesn't want—' She closed her mouth and
stared, stony-faced, out of the window, conscious of
James's quick sideways glance as he drew to a halt
at a set of traffic lights.

'Beth?' he prompted.

She took a deep breath. Oh, what the heck? 'I had
a letter from my aunt a few days ago,' she said ex-
pressionlessly. 'She's invited a recently widowed
schoolfriend to stay for Christmas.'

'So?'

'It's a small cottage...only two bedrooms. There
isn't a lot of room...' Beth knew how lame it
sounded—as lame as it had sounded when she'd read
the stark words. 'Of course you could always sleep
on the sofa, I suppose' her aunt had added grudgingly,
evidently hoping she wouldn't take her up on the offer.

She was aware of the silence in the car and flicked
James a cautious glance, flinching at the compassion
in his eyes, knowing that he had guessed at much that

she'd left unsaid. The last thing she wanted was for him or anyone else to feel sorry for her.

'Why didn't you tell me?' he said quietly, inching the car forward as the lights changed to green.

She shrugged. She hadn't told anyone. Partly pride, she supposed. And partly because she hadn't wanted to put any of her friends in the difficult position of feeling obligated to ask her to spend Christmas with their families. Besides, she hadn't even known until five days ago that she was going to be spending a solitary Christmas.

Her initial hurt at her aunt's letter had now given way to an overwhelming sadness at the realisation of just how far apart they had both grown. She'd also been honest enough to accept that she was partly responsible for that widening gulf. She would go and visit Aunt Mary in the new year, she suddenly decided resolutely. Or maybe persuade her to come up to London for the weekend...

'So Timmy and I are going to be stuck with you over Christmas.'

She stiffened as James's teasing voice broke through her thoughts.

'No,' she said abruptly. She wasn't going to spend Christmas with him because he felt *sorry* for her.

'So what are you proposing to do?' he drawled.

'I haven't decided yet,' she returned nonchalantly, the implication being that she was spoiled for choice! But instead of being relieved when he made no attempt to pursue the matter she was perversely disappointed. She was open to persuasion!

How was he planning to spend the two days anyway? Presumably he usually spent some of the time with his family, but that was somewhat depleted this year with both his parents and two of his sisters out of the country.

She flicked a swift glance at the silent man by her side, and her heart constricted painfully. Blast her stupid, ridiculous pride. There was nothing she wanted more than to wake up on Christmas morning and see Timmy and James. She chewed her lip.

'Um, James...?'

'Mmm?'

Courage deserted her. 'It's snowing now,' she said brightly, and heard his soft chuckle as he turned left into a side street and drew to a smooth halt in a parking space.

He knew exactly what she'd been trying to say, knew she'd changed her mind.

'Thank you,' she murmured coolly a few moments later as James opened the passenger door, and turned up her coat collar against the falling snow as she joined him on the pavement.

'It's settling.' James glanced at the rooftops on the other side of the street then grinned down into Beth's face.

Her stomach dipping, Beth grinned back, everything else forgotten as anticipation tingled through her. 'I can't remember the last time we had a white Christmas.' She had James to herself for the whole evening and she was going to savour every single second of it. 'And that's not a cue,' she added with mock severity.

'You're a hard woman, Beth Sinclair,' he said solemnly as he stooped to lock the car. Pocketing the keys, he guided her the few yards to the restaurant.

'Good evening, Mr Fenner.' The *maître d'* immediately broke off his conversation with an immaculately attired waiter and moved noiselessly across the thick carpet to greet them.

'Good evening, Mark,' James returned easily, exchanging smiles with the young woman who appeared from nowhere and whisked Beth's coat away to the cloakroom.

So James was evidently a regular patron, Beth registered, trying not to speculate on whom his companions had been on those other occasions as she glanced around the candlelit, damask-covered tables, most of which were occupied by couples. Who cared? It was tonight that mattered!

'The rest of your party's already arrived,' the *maître d'* murmured over his shoulder as he turned to lead them through the restaurant.

Beth stiffened, aware of the light touch of James's hand on her elbow. 'What party?'

'It's my grandmother's birthday,' he returned blandly.

'What?' Her eyes shot to his face, disbelief turning to steadily mounting anger. 'You mean it's a family celebration?' She was aware that his hand had tightened on her arm as if he feared she might turn round and bolt. 'Why didn't you tell me?' she demanded.

'Because you probably wouldn't have come,' he said equably.

'I would have liked to have had the choice,' she bit back. How dared he spring this on her without any warning? Her eyes darkened with apprehension as she saw the group of complete strangers gathered around the oval table ahead of them. She'd just about managed to psyche herself up to cope with James this evening—but his family as well...

And that beautifully groomed woman sitting in the centre beside the distinguished grey-haired man, who had risen courteously to his feet at their approach, looked positively terrifying—certainly not a white-haired, pink-cheeked granny.

Amid cries of greeting, James stooped to kiss the formidable woman. 'Happy birthday,' he murmured and, straightening up, introduced Beth.

As she shook the extended, bejewelled hand, Beth was conscious that the faded but still astute blue eyes which had sparked with recognition at her name were now inspecting her with unveiled curiosity.

No doubt James's grandmother was as startled by the inclusion of her grandson's secretary in the birthday celebrations as Beth was herself. She felt like a gatecrasher. How could James put her in this position? Terrified she might explode, she studiously avoided looking at him as he continued with the introductions, the nameless faces slowly taking on identities.

James's grandfather, his brown eyes warm and humorous. The twins, Becky and Ruth, distinguishable from each other only by the differing lengths of their dark hair, their expressive, mobile faces identical. Anna, slightly plumper than her younger sisters, her eyes the same vivid blue as James's sitting beside her pleasant-faced husband.

Her jaw beginning to ache with the fixed smile, Beth sat down as the waiter drew out a chair for her opposite James, in between his grandfather and Ruth. Presumably James had telephoned the restaurant earlier and made an addition to the booking, so at least she was spared the embarrassment of the waiter discreetly laying up an extra table-setting right in front of her eyes.

'Would you like a drink, Beth?' James enquired.

A treble brandy. 'Mineral water, please,' she answered, still refusing to look at him, the attentive, solicitous note in his voice perversely making her seethe even more. 'Thank you,' she murmured as the waiter handed her a menu.

'I'm starving,' Ruth announced on Beth's left, and added softly with an impish grin, 'Have you and James just had a row? You looked as if you wanted to throttle him just now!'

Startled by the other girl's directness, Beth was saved the necessity for a reply as Ruth continued, unabashed, 'The number of times I've felt like doing that myself!' Her words were belied by the affectionate glance she threw at her brother, who was talking to their grandparents.

'When Becky and I were in our early teens, Mum sometimes accompanied Dad on tours with the orchestra...' Ruth leant forward confidentially '...leaving us in the big brother's tender care.' Her face took on an expression of mock horror. 'It was like living with a prison warder!

'Hey, Beck,' she called to her twin who was sitting opposite. 'Do you remember that time when we were seventeen and we went to a party and James insisted on collecting us—?'

'At ten o'clock!' Becky chipped in with a groan.

'And what about that time when—?'

'I really don't think Beth is interested in family anecdotes,' James's deep voice cut in crisply.

Oh, but she was! Beth exchanged grins with the twins. Absolutely fascinated.

'How's Timmy, James?' Anna asked. 'I really don't know why you insist on employing a nanny for him when I'd be more than happy to look after him now I've finished those recording sessions.'

'And Becky and I wouldn't mind a chance to play doting aunties either now we've broken up for the holidays,' Ruth joined in.

'Nephew-hogger!' Becky put in amiably.

Now this was getting even more interesting! Beth nearly choked on her mineral water. Not only were James's family under the impression that he was employing a professional nanny, but it was also evident that there was no need for him to have done so anyway. So why exactly was she living in his flat, minding Timmy, when three of his aunts were practically fighting to have him?

Looking across the table at James, she raised her eyebrows and smiled sweetly.

He smiled back, unperturbed. 'Timmy is settled where he is,' he informed his sisters in a voice that clearly brooked no argument. 'Now, is everyone ready to order?'

Beth joined in the burst of laughter as James solemnly concluded the hilarious, highly improbable tale with which he'd been regaling them.

'I don't believe a word of it,' Ruth scoffed with a grin, and returned enthusiastically to the rich, cream-covered chocolate gateau on her plate.

'What shall we try next?' James's grandfather turned to Beth with twinkling brown eyes.

They'd both opted for the cheese board instead of a dessert from the sweet trolley, and were now companionably sampling and commenting on the unusual and wide selection on offer.

'The one with the walnut and orange looks interesting,' Beth decided, picking up the cheese knife and slicing off two thin slivers. With the gravity of wine connoisseurs they swallowed their respective morsels, looked at each other consideringly for a moment and then both nodded approvingly.

'Another biscuit, Beth?'

'Thank you.' Beth accepted a cracker from the proffered basket, her liking for the gentle, courteous man increasing as the evening wore on. In fact she liked all of James's warm, affectionate family, she admitted—even the family matriarch had proved less daunting on further acquaintance.

Surreptitiously Beth stole a glance at James from under her lashes, watching the candlelight flicker over the planes of his face. The temptation to keep looking at him had become increasingly hard to resist. And it wasn't only James from whom she had to hide that compulsion—the last thing she wanted was a knowing, cheeky grin from Ruth!

'Beth...'

Her stomach muscles suddenly cramped as, mesmerised, she watched James lick off a tiny smear of cream from his upper lip.

'Would you pass the water, please?'

'Um, yes. Sorry.' Swiftly averting her gaze, Beth absently passed the jug to Anna, and with horror realised that everybody's eyes—except James's—were upon her. How long had she been staring, transfixed, at him? The very thing she'd vowed not to do in front of this all too observant gathering! And that grin on Ruth's face was exactly the one she'd dreaded.

With a nonchalance she was far from feeling, Beth finished off her cheese and biscuit, glad when the general buzz of conversation resumed around her.

'How are you spending Christmas, my dear?' James's grandmother asked casually, folding up her napkin.

The question had been inevitable sooner or later, Beth supposed. She smiled at the older woman, suddenly conscious of James watching her. 'I'm—'

'Beth's spending Christmas with me.' The deep, drawling voice overrode hers.

Was she indeed? With excruciating embarrassment, Beth saw the swiftly concealed surprise in the faded blue eyes as they flicked to James and then back towards her.

'Then you'll be joining us for lunch on Christmas Day. I shall look forward to it, my dear.'

'Thank you.' Beth forced the words out, aware that, however graciously it had been couched, the other woman had had no choice other than to include Beth in the invitation that had obviously already been extended to her grandson.

Hands clenched into fists in her lap, Beth's furious eyes darted to the dark face opposite her.

'Coffee?' he enquired of the table at large, seemingly oblivious to her glare.

'Actually, darling...' his grandmother exchanged a glance with her husband '...I think we'll pass. It's been a lovely evening...' Leaning over, she kissed

James on the cheek. 'No, don't get up,' she added, rising to her feet as her husband drew back her chair.

'I think we'd better make a move too.' Anna and her husband followed suit.

'And Becky and I have promised to look in at a party,' Ruth announced. 'The meal was scrumptious, James. Thanks.'

It all happened so quickly that before Beth really had time to register what was happening the party had dispersed and she was left alone with James.

'That was a lousy, stinking thing to do!' No longer inhibited by his family's presence, she finally exploded. 'You gave your grandmother no option other than to invite me for Christmas lunch. It wasn't damn well fair on either of us.' Automatically she muttered her thanks as the waiter placed a coffee in front of her.

'I think you're jumping to conclusions, Beth. As usual,' James murmured mildly, taking an appreciative sip from his own cup. 'As it happens I'm the one who's invited you to lunch. Normally we all go to my parents', but this year Anna's going to her in-laws and the twins and my grandparents are coming to me.'

'What?' Beth stared at him. 'You're cooking the Christmas dinner?' she snorted in disbelief, trying to recall exactly what his grandmother had said.

'The twins insisted that we draw straws for the honour.' He suddenly grinned. 'And I lost.'

Despite herself Beth grinned back, envisaging Ruth and Becky's staunch declaration that the task shouldn't automatically fall to them by virtue of their sex.

'Fortunately,' he added, his grin broadening, 'I happen to know an excellent outside catering firm.'

'That's cheating,' Beth admonished him, her heart squeezing as her eyes locked with his. How was she supposed to stay angry and resentful when he looked at her like that? Warmth scudded through her in little waves.

'Have you enjoyed tonight?' he asked softly, without breaking his gaze.

'Yes,' she admitted honestly. He didn't even have to touch her, could reduce her to putty just by looking at her. 'But it was still a lousy thing to do...' she mumbled without much conviction, no longer able to recapture her original anger. 'Why didn't you simply—?'

'Ask you if you'd like to have dinner with my family?' He raised a dark eyebrow. 'Because you wouldn't have given me a straight yes or no,' he said dryly. 'You would have surveyed me with those large, suspicious eyes and immediately demanded to know why!'

'Of course I wouldn't,' she denied untruthfully. And she still wanted to know why. Her eyes moved over his face. His sisters might have the same dark hair and blue eyes, but the strong, carved features were uniquely his own. 'Your family's very important to you, isn't it?' she said quietly.

'Yes,' he answered simply.

Her eyes dropped to her cup and discovered it was empty—as empty as she suddenly felt inside. To whom was she important?

'Stop feeling sorry for yourself!'

Colour washing over her face, Beth jerked her head

up. 'I wasn't!' she said furiously. He had the sensitivity of a brick wall—couldn't possibly understand...

'Yes, I know,' he said dryly. 'I couldn't possibly understand what it's like to be virtually all alone in the world. Especially at Christmas,' he finished sardonically.

Beth's lips curved involuntarily. She hadn't got around to being quite that maudlin!

'If you want a family,' he continued crisply, 'do something about it. Get married. Have children.'

'Just like that?' she scoffed, a stab of hurt tearing through her at the knowledge that he obviously wouldn't care if she did.

'You'd make a good mother,' he said unexpectedly, his eyes unreadable beneath the sweep of jet-black lashes.

She tried to think of some flip rejoinder, but her mind was blank, the glow of pleasure his words had given her instantly dulling the hurt. And you, she thought, her eyes resting on the dark face, would make a wonderful father. Dangerous ground, she warned herself, dropping her gaze.

'Would you like another coffee?'

As Beth shook her head, James glanced at his wristwatch and summoned the waiter. 'I promised Mrs Andrews we wouldn't be too late.' He settled the bill and, rising to his feet, helped Beth on with her coat, which had appeared as unobtrusively as it had vanished, and ushered her towards the door.

It was still snowing as they stepped out into the still night, large flakes drifting slowly down from the darkened sky.

'It's so quiet,' Beth murmured softly, aware of

James's steadying hand on her arm as they walked along the pavement to the car, and then grinned wryly as the sound of a band spilled out noisily from the pub on the corner.

'Shall we?'

Catching her completely by surprise, James swung Beth around in front of him, his hand dropping to her waist as he skilfully directed her movements to match his.

This was utterly absurd. Beth laughed up into the dark face as they whirled in time to the fast beat of the music, the warmth from the firm fingers clasping her hand charging up her arm in tiny shock waves. Dancing on a London pavement in the snow. Her eyes shone with the sheer exuberance of being alive.

The mood and the tempo of the music changed, a lone guitarist picking out a slow, haunting tune. Gently James drew Beth further into the circle of his arms, his jaw brushing her silky hair as her head fell against his muscled shoulder. Their warm breath mingling in the night air, they swayed slowly together on the white, deserted pavement.

She would remember this moment for as long as she lived. Lost in a web of enchantment, Beth closed her eyes as she nestled against James, melting into him. Vaguely she was aware that both the music and the snow had stopped, and that they had come to a standstill.

She gave a tiny little sigh as she felt the touch of James's lips on her temple, and tilted her face towards him. He looked back down at her with dark, drowsy, half-closed eyes and slowly lowered his head.

There was no explosion of senses as his mouth

closed over hers, just a languorous spiral of hypnotic pleasure. As he lifted his head, she smiled dreamily up at him and gently brushed the errant lock of dark hair from his forehead, her heart twisting as her eyes moved caressingly over the hard, rugged planes of his face.

If anyone ever hurt this man, made him un-happy…if anything should ever happen to him… The intensity of the emotion tearing through her nearly made her cry out in pain. Her eyes blurring with tears, her hands tightened round his neck as she reached up and kissed him with a fierce, desperate urgency.

Oh, God! What was she doing? She heard James's sharp intake of breath as she wrenched her mouth from his, but didn't wait to see the expression on his face. Spinning away, she headed blindly down the pavement.

'Beth!' He caught up with her as she reached the car, and grabbed hold of her shoulders. 'What the hell's the matter?' he demanded.

'Nothing!' She flung off his restraining hand. Nothing except that she'd just made a complete and utter fool of herself.

'Oh, Beth, darling.' With a sudden low chuckle he caught hold of her again.

'Would you—?'

'Unhand me, sir?' he enquired, mimicking her frigid tone, and with another chuckle swung her round and hugged her. 'You're not living in Victorian England, Beth. It's quite socially acceptable for a woman to invite a man out these days, even make the first move…'

'What? I was not making a move on you!' she

denied furiously, and then her mouth began to curve
unwillingly as she saw the laughter in his eyes. She
had slightly overreacted, hadn't she? Which had probably been the biggest give-away of all, she thought
wryly. Had he really called her 'darling' just now?
And what exactly was she doing in his arms again?

His eyes locking with hers, James lifted a hand and
traced the contours of her face. Cupping her chin in
his palm, his thumb and fingers brushed her lips and
moved in slow, sensuous circles over her jaw and the
top of her throat.

'You're shivering...' he muttered gruffly, and, releasing her, swiftly unlocked the car and opened the
door. 'Come on, get in,' he ordered.

Obediently, Beth slipped into the passenger seat,
her head falling back weakly against the head-rest as
she dazedly watched James clearing the snow from
the windows. What exactly was happening between
her and James? And more to the point, she thought
with a long shudder, where did they go from here?

She tensed as James opened the driver's door and
folded his long frame into the seat beside her. 'Your
safety belt's twisted,' he told her casually, automatically stretching out an arm to rectify it.

'I can manage,' she mumbled, shrinking away as
his hand brushed her shoulder. She saw his eyebrows
draw together, and then, before she could help herself,
blurted out, 'I don't want to start some casual, meaningless affair with you, James.'

If he'd laughed, told her that was the furthest thing
from his mind, told her that she'd completely misread
the male signals, it would have been bad enough. But
the long, protracted silence was even worse.

'And you think that's what I want,' he said finally, his voice cool and remote.

'I don't know what you want...' she muttered. She was completely out of her depth; she wished she'd never started this. Damn it all! This situation wasn't of her making; she wasn't the one who'd first crossed the professional line between them. She couldn't just switch on and off like him, couldn't just wake up tomorrow and play the dutiful employee again. She turned to him, her eyes blazing, her anger intensified by the cold indifference on his face.

'I'm your secretary!' The warmth, the tenderness, the gentleness he'd shown her tonight had meant absolutely nothing. It had all been part of a well-polished, much practised act performed by an expert.

'So you persist in reminding me,' he said curtly, and then suddenly slammed his fists on the steering wheel. 'Don't you think I damn well know you're my secretary? Do you think I'm likely to forget it?' he thundered, his eyes raking over her shocked face.

She'd never seen James exhibit any extremes of emotion, had never known him to lose his temper before. He might get angry, impatient, but he was always totally in control.

Silently she watched as, grim-faced, he switched on the ignition, the car moving smoothly away from the kerb and turning left into the slow-moving traffic at the end of the street. It was impossible to believe that only a few short minutes ago she'd been in the arms of this chilling, forbidding stranger.

She jerked her head back to the front, her mouth tightening mutinously as she stared unseeingly out of the window. She was sick to death of his mood swings, sick to death of the way he kept blowing hot and cold.

It was some time later before it occurred to her that she might very well be guilty of the same crime.

'He's been an angel.' Taking a sip from her glass, Mrs Andrews settled herself more comfortably on the sofa and smiled across the lounge at Beth. 'Not a peep out of him all night.'

Beth smiled back, suppressing the urge to open her mouth and scream, wondering how on earth the other woman could be so completely oblivious to the tension in the room. It wasn't that she didn't like Mrs Andrews—of course she did. And at any other time she would have been more than happy to listen to the older woman extolling Timmy's virtues. But right now she just wanted with all her being to escape to her room. She craved bed, to close her eyes and blank out James.

She flicked him a glance from under her eyelashes as he sat in the armchair opposite her, long legs sprawled out in front of him, nursing a whisky in his hand. What on earth had possessed him to invite Mrs Andrews to join them for a nightcap, deliberately prolonging this disastrous evening?

Cursing him soundly under her breath, she stared down at the amber liquid in her glass. She didn't even like brandy, had no idea why she'd blithely asked for one just now.

'Well, I'd better make a move or Dan will be wondering where I am.' Mrs Andrews drained her glass and stood up.

'I'll see you back to your flat.' Ignoring her protests

that it was unnecessary, James rose swiftly to his feet and courteously ushered the plump, good-natured woman from the room. Muffling her relief, Beth trooped after them to the front door.

'Goodnight, Mrs Andrews.' After watching them disappear into the lift, Beth closed the front door and expelled a long breath before hurrying down the hall. Just a quick check on Timmy and then with any luck she'd be safely ensconced in her bedroom by the time James returned.

Was there anything more therapeutic than looking at a sleeping baby? she wondered a few moments later, feeling the tension drain from her body as she gazed into the cot. Her eyes softening, she very gently extracted the thumb from Timmy's mouth and straightened his cover, the urge to pick him up and hug him almost irresistible.

Smiling gently, she turned away from the cot, her smile instantly fading as she saw James towering in the doorway watching her. She hadn't heard him return.

'Timmy's asleep,' she said unnecessarily as he stood aside to let her pass into the hall.

'I want to talk to you,' he said abruptly.

'I'm tired,' she said coolly. He hadn't spoken one word, not one lousy word to her in the car on the trip back to the flat, and now he wanted to talk? Too bad. 'It'll have to wait until tomorrow.'

'No,' he said firmly and, taking hold of her arm, propelled her back down the hall and into the lounge. 'Sit down.'

She hesitated and then, shrugging, did as he asked.

'Well?' she enquired shortly as he sat down in the leather armchair opposite her.

'I want you to resign as my secretary,' he said quietly.

For a second she was too stunned to even think, and then she jumped furiously to her feet. 'Are you sacking me?' she demanded.

'Of course I'm—'

'On what grounds?' Her eyes narrowed with outraged disbelief. 'Because I won't have a quick fling with the boss?'

'Don't be so damn ridiculous—'

'I'll sue you...unfair dismissal...sexual harassment...'

'If you'd just damn well shut up for two seconds and listen...'

'You'll wake Timmy if you keep bellowing like that...and don't tell me—'

'Will you marry me, Beth?' James's voice thundered round the room as she paused to draw breath.

CHAPTER EIGHT

WEAKLY Beth slumped back down into her chair, staring incredulously at James. She couldn't have heard him correctly. She was dreaming. It was a sick joke. Her eyes moved over the dark face. He was deadly serious.

'I don't expect you to give me an answer tonight,' he said quietly.

She couldn't have given him an answer right now even if she'd wanted to. Desperately Beth tried to stop the bubble of hysteria rising in her throat. This simply could not be happening. It was all wrong.

Admittedly her experience of these matters was somewhat limited, having received her first and only other proposal when she was six. But surely proposals of marriage weren't normally preceded by a shouting match? And at this point in time surely she should be in James's arms, listening to his tender endearments and avowals of eternal love? Instead of which they were both surveying each other across the room as if the only thing on the agenda were the weather.

She swallowed hard. 'So you want me to trade in being your secretary to become your wife?' She just couldn't take this seriously...just couldn't. 'Is that a promotion?'

She saw a muscle flicker along the line of his jaw. 'Stop being flip, Beth.'

She swallowed again, her heart beginning to hammer so loudly she was sure he must hear it. 'Why do you want to marry me, James? You don't love me,' she stated flatly, and her stomach cramped, hoping against all reason that he would instantly refute the statement.

He didn't. For a moment he didn't say anything. He simply sat back in his chair and surveyed her with fathomless blue eyes.

'I like having you in the flat,' he finally said evenly. 'I like coming home and finding you and Timmy here.'

Beth's throat constricted, warmth flooding through her. 'Do you?' she said unsteadily, her hands gripping the arms of the chair to restrain herself from crossing the room and launching herself into his arms.

'I want a wife, Beth,' he said quietly. 'Children.'

She froze, comprehension dawning in her wide hazel eyes. He didn't want her, Beth Sinclair—merely a woman to bear his name and his children. 'And you think that I just might fit the vacancy? Make a suitable mother for your children?' she enquired conversationally, her fingers aching as her grip on the chair grew tighter and tighter. Go to hell, James, she seethed silently. 'Is that why you wanted me to meet your family tonight? To get their approval first?'

The dark eyebrows drew together. 'Don't be so ridiculous, Beth.'

She knew she was being ridiculous, knew that James Fenner would never seek or need anyone's approval but his own, but she didn't care. 'Or was it to show me what I'd get out of this deal—or should I call it a merger? A ready-made extended family?' Her childhood dream... 'As well as presumably all the financial advantages of being married to a wealthy man. And what would happen if I didn't conceive a child within the allotted time? A quickie divorce and a replacement in your bed?'

'Now you're being utterly absurd!'

'And you're not? Asking me to marry you because you've a sudden whim to have a child?' She took a deep, controlling breath. 'Sorry, James, you've nothing to offer me that I want,' she said steadily. 'I don't need to get married for financial security. I've a career. I don't even need to get married to have a child.' Not that she would for one moment ever consider voluntary single parenthood, but it had been worth saying just to see the flicker of surprise—or was it disapproval?—in his eyes.

'I should prefer you to give up working, Beth, but I wouldn't insist on it.'

Beth stared at him. He wouldn't insist on it? Hadn't he heard a word she'd been saying? Did he think her job was the stumbling block? That her career was that important to her? How could he know so little about her? Didn't he know that if he loved her she would give up everything and anything for him?

Slowly she forced herself to her feet. 'Get a dog or cat if you want something to welcome you home at night,' she advised coolly.

He lifted a dark eyebrow. 'Do I take that as a no?' he drawled, leaning back indolently in his chair.

She didn't even bother to answer. Summoning every ounce of control, she walked calmly towards the door. Her rejection hadn't even dented his male ego, let alone inflicted a deeper wound. But then why should it? He wasn't in love with her, and she didn't doubt for a moment that he would have no trouble finding some other woman to play happy families with him.

Reaching her room, she crossed to the window, drew back the curtains and gazed out into the silent white world. So why hadn't he asked one of those other women? Why not Julia? Why her?

Turning away from the window, she kicked off her shoes and sat on the bed, clasping her arms round her legs, knees drawn up to her chin. The whole thing was incomprehensible. James was incomprehensible. It was the most ludicrous thing she'd ever heard in her life. Laughable. She sniffed, and dashed a hand across her cheek. So why exactly was she crying?

She swung her legs back onto the carpet, slipped on her shoes and crossed to the door. Opening it silently, she peeped down the hall. Good. James's bedroom door was firmly closed. Noiselessly she crept down to the kitchen.

She heated some milk, poured it into a mug and carried it over to the table, together with a packet of instant-chocolate sachets. Stirring the contents of one of the sachets into her mug, she stared down into the brown depths. Hot chocolate. Soothing. Comforting. She pulled a wry face. And a substitute for what? Love? Sex? Her lips began to tremble. Love might not have been included in James's marriage package, but presumably sex would have been pretty high on the agenda!

She began to shake with convulsive giggles. In fact, on reflection she was surprised he hadn't mentioned that particular advantage of becoming Mrs Fenner.

The laughter froze on her lips at the mental picture

exploding in her head. Lying in bed next to that warm, hard, male body. Feeling his mouth. His hands moving expertly, knowingly over her bare skin, preparing her for that moment of final, irrevocable intimacy. But they wouldn't be making love, they would be having sex. A wave of revulsion shuddered over her. Their child wouldn't be conceived out of mutual love but would be the end product of an unemotional, fundamental biological process.

She just couldn't believe that James could seriously think that she would even consider, let alone agree to, such a cold-blooded union. She chewed her lip, her eyes darkening. And would he really want a marriage completely devoid of all affection?

Maybe she had overreacted, hadn't given him a fair chance. James might not love her, but surely he must at least like her, as well as presumably feeling a degree of physical attraction for her. That might not be the soundest of foundations for a marriage, but it was a start. And he might not love her, but he couldn't love anyone else either, could he?

She brought herself up sharply, taking a swift gulp from her mug. Don't even think it. Forget it. Forget the whole...

She nearly choked as the door opened and James, still clad in his white shirt and dark trousers, strode in. Nodding to her absently, he crossed the kitchen, switched on the kettle and, whistling softly between his teeth, calmly spooned coffee into a mug.

Beth stared at the broad, muscular back, averting her eyes the moment he turned round. As he walked over to the table, armed with his coffee, she swiftly picked up her own mug again and avidly began to read the labelling on the packet in front of her: if she collected the tops from six packets of instant hot chocolate, she could send off for a free place-mat.

Cautiously Beth raised her head. Sitting down opposite her, James casually retrieved the newspaper from the stool beside him and began to glance through it idly as he drank his coffee.

Surreptitiously her eyes flicked to his face, and learned absolutely nothing from the impassive mask. But then when had she ever known what was going on inside that dark head? Ever known what he was really thinking…feeling…?

If she collected the tops from twelve packets she could send off for a free tray. Warily Beth glanced up again. How could James just sit there, relaxed and at ease, flipping through that paper? Damn it all, he'd asked her to have his child!

Picking up her spoon, she stirred the contents of her mug vigorously. This time as she looked up she was trapped by a pair of dark blue eyes. Jet-black eyebrows rose inquiringly.

She shrugged.

The blue eyes moved slowly over her face then dropped thoughtfully to her tightly compressed mouth.

The spoon slipped from Beth's grasp and went clattering across the table towards James; the sound seemed deafening in the silent kitchen.

Smiling blandly, James retrieved the spoon and handed it back to her, his long, supple fingers brushing against her outstretched palm.

Abruptly Beth pushed back her chair and rose to her feet. Picking up her mug, she dumped it in the sink and then headed for the door. The minute she was out in the hall she stopped and aimed a ferocious kick at the skirting-board, wincing as she stubbed her toe.

Then, seeing the imprint of her shoe on the pristine white paint, she stooped down and began rubbing it guiltily with her fingers. Catching a movement out of the corner of her eye, she stiffened and glanced over her shoulder.

James, arms folded across his broad chest, was leaning idly against the kitchen door-jamb, watching her with interest.

With great dignity, Beth rose to her feet and continued on down the hall. To hell with James. To hell with everything.

Bleary-eyed, Beth tossed back the duvet and fumbled for the switch on her beside lamp.

'Coming, Timmy,' she mumbled under her breath as the tiny wails increased determinedly in volume. She peered at her wristwatch, sweeping her tumbled hair back over her shoulders. Seven o'clock. She groaned. It couldn't be morning—not already.

Acting on auto-pilot, she scrambled out of bed and reached for her dressing gown, securing it round her waist as she padded across the room to the door. Giving her bed one last, envious look, she made her way down the hall, faltering as she saw James emerge from his room. Bare-chested and bare-foot, he was muffling a yawn as he fastened the belt on his jeans.

She cursed ferociously under her breath. She needed another four or five hours' sleep and a gallon of tea before she could cope with that hard male torso with any degree of equanimity. James, judging from that frown of vague recognition on his face, seemed equally thrilled to see her.

Raking a hand through his dark, tousled hair, he grunted something incomprehensible and, turning away, strode in the direction of the kitchen.

Perhaps she and James were never actually going to hold a normal conversation again. Which on reflection might not be such a bad thing, Beth decided grouchily as she sped into Timmy's room. He stopped crying the moment she picked him up, but his large, reproachful eyes informed her sadly that he wasn't totally satisfied with her response time.

'I came as quickly as I could,' Beth protested defensively, unfastening his buttons.

Relenting, he beamed at her and patted her cheek.

'But don't think everyone's going to jump around you for the rest of your life,' she warned him. 'Unfortunately some people have been known to make that mistake.'

He looked up at her soberly as she laid him down on the plastic sheet on the bed—hopefully, Beth mused, taking her advice to heart.

Her technique was definitely improving, she decided with satisfaction a short time later as she sat on the edge of the bed with a freshly changed Timmy on her lap. She was about to stand up when James walked in, balancing a tray with Timmy's bottle and two mugs of tea on it.

Placing the tray on the bedside table, he handed her the bottle, which was greeted eagerly by the small, waiting mouth and flapping hands.

'Thank you,' Beth muttered, her stomach lurching

as she looked up at James, her sense of smell assaulted by the warm, sleepy male scent of him. His jaw was shadowed, the stubble as dark as the silky hairs that trailed down his chest, over the taut, flat stomach and disappeared beneath the waistband of his jeans.

For one awful moment as he stooped to pick up one of the mugs she thought he was going to sit down on the bed beside her to drink his tea, but then, to her relief, he turned and walked out of the door.

What a way to start the day, Beth thought gloomily as she looked down at Timmy—her composure shot to pieces before it was even light outside. As he nestled against her trustingly, Timmy's eyes half closed and he sucked contentedly on his bottle. If she married James, she would become Timmy's aunt...

Just drop it, she ordered herself wearily, taking a swift gulp of tea as Timmy paused for breath. She couldn't even think straight any more after the mental battering she'd given herself during her restless, sleepless night.

Setting the empty bottle on the table, she wiped Timmy's milky chin and looked up as James re-entered the room, his hair damp from the shower, a dark green sweatshirt hugging his broad shoulders.

'I'll see to Timmy's breakfast if you want to get showered and dressed.'

So he hadn't taken a vow of silence after all. Rising to her feet, Beth passed Timmy into the strong, gentle hands, very conscious of the blue eyes sweeping over her milk-splattered dressing gown and dishevelled hair.

'Take your time,' he drawled generously.

'Thank you,' she said sweetly. She fully intended
to.

'Right, Timmy, what do you fancy for breakfast
this morning? Eggs, bacon, tomatoes, fried bread?'
the deep voice murmured behind her as she crossed
towards the door. 'Hmm? A couple of sausages *too*?
Now that is overdoing it, old chap.'

Absently folding back the sleeves of her pink sweater,
Beth walked across to the French windows and stared
out despondently at the falling snow. The white world
that had so entranced her last night had completely
lost its enchantment. What was she going to do,
trapped here in the flat with James all day, unable
even to escape for a walk with Timmy?

It would be too much to hope that James would go
into the office on a snowy Sunday two days before
Christmas, she supposed, sighing inwardly. She gave
him a sideways glance. By the look of him he had no
plans to go anywhere. Evincing none of her own tension, he was sitting on the sofa with Timmy on his
lap, long legs sprawled out idly in front of him, pen
in hand, studying the crossword in the Sunday paper.

He'd made no reference to his proposal today, as
if he'd completely dismissed it from his mind. Unobserved, Beth's eyes swept over the dark face, coming
to rest on the square chin. For a man with such de-
termination he seemed to have accepted her refusal
very readily, had evidently no intention of persuading
her to change her mind.

Which rather indicated, she admitted with painful
honesty, that the proposal had been made on the spur
of the moment, in a rare moment of weakness induced

by tiredness, the lateness of the hour, the sudden desire for a family of his own. Probably, in the cold light of day, he had been overwhelmingly relieved that she hadn't accepted, had realised himself just how disastrous it would be to tie himself to a woman he didn't love.

Walking over to the Christmas tree, she rearranged a strand of tinsel. Even the tree had lost its magic this morning. She turned away.

'You're not a prisoner, Beth.' Abruptly James lifted his head and surveyed her across the room. 'You're perfectly free to walk out of the flat any time you choose,' he said quietly.

Caught completely off balance, Beth stiffened, searching his face. 'Do you want me to go?' she asked jerkily.

'Do you want to go?' His eyes sought and held hers.

She swallowed, aware of an uncharacteristic capriciousness inside her encouraging her to say yes, just to see his reaction, to see if he attempted to dissuade her. But it was a risk she couldn't afford to take; it might well backfire on her. And neither did she really want to play infantile games with him.

'No,' she said honestly, and saw his eyes flicker, but with what emotion it was impossible to say. If only, she thought with a swirl of frustration, he would just show his feelings occasionally. He must care something for her. Or was she just deluding herself completely?

'Your flat's much warmer than mine,' she added quickly, and then began to grin reluctantly. He knew perfectly well why she wanted to stay, and it had nothing to do with the temperature of her flat.

'I must admit it would be inconvenient if you walked out on me now,' James returned thoughtfully, and his own mouth began to quirk. 'I'd much prefer it if you came and sat here—' he patted the seat beside him '—and helped me with this crossword, because my nephew's contribution has been absolutely zilch so far.'

Beth's grin widened, warmth bubbling through her. Suddenly it felt as if he didn't want her to stay just to help with a few cryptic clues, or even because of Timmy.

'I think your nephew is either deep in meditation or having a sneaky nap,' she observed, and with a casualness she was far from feeling sat down beside James. 'Shall I pop him in his cot?'

'He's fine where he is,' James drawled easily, his left hand tightening round the sleeping infant flopped against the crook of his shoulder.

'Three across,' he instructed, rearranging the news-paper across his knee.

Obediently Beth bowed her head over the paper, her curtain of hair concealing her face as she consci-entiously studied the lean, firm fingers holding the pen.

'I think it's probably an anagram,' James mur-mured.

'Yes,' she agreed. Her eyes rested on the expanse of strong, tanned wrist visible below the cuff of the green sweatshirt.

'You're not concentrating, Beth,' a deep voice ad-monished her close to her ear.

And neither are you, James Fenner! Beth tilted her head upwards and looked into the dark face only inches away from hers. 'Do you always do crosswords upside down?' she asked innocently.

'More of a challenge,' he said airily. Casually he lifted a hand and tucked a lock of silky hair behind her ear, the deep blue eyes moving slowly over her face. 'And if you're planning to go on looking at me like that,' he added conversationally, 'it might be an idea to put Timmy in his cot after all.'

'Looking at you like what?' Beth enquired, the warmth escalating inside her as his fingers traced the delicate whorls of her ear and slid slowly down to her throat.

'With that come-hither expression.' His head lowered towards her.

The conceited rat! 'I was not...' Beth's words were muffled as his mouth closed gently over hers, a little sigh escaping her as he lifted his head.

'Timmy,' they both murmured simultaneously, exchanging grins as they looked at him.

Wide awake, he was surveying them both with large, disapproving blue eyes.

'Well, I can't sit here all day dallying with you, Ms Sinclair.' Glancing out of the window, James rose energetically to his feet, and placed his nephew on his activity mat. 'I have a pressing matter to attend to now it's stopped snowing.' Briskly he strode towards the door.

Beth's eyes followed him in bewilderment. What pressing matter? Her bewilderment changed to sudden suspicion as he returned a few moments later clad in a waxed jacket and wielding a small spade.

'Promised Tim I'd make him a snowman,' he drawled laconically, crossing towards the French window.

'And you should always keep a promise to a child,' she returned gravely, sliding the door closed behind him as he stepped out onto the white balcony.

Snorting with laughter, Beth gathered Timmy up in her arms and carried him across to the window. A pale sun was beginning to break through the grey cloud.

'Humour him, Tim,' she whispered into a tiny ear. Obligingly Timmy waved his small arms enthusiastically in the air, his eyes round with fascination as he watched his uncle shovelling snow into a small mound.

'At least we can't *hear* him whistling!'

As if on cue, James glanced up with a grin, inviting her in sign language to join him.

'Looks like your uncle needs our advice.' Beth's breath caught in her throat as she met James's dazzling eyes through the glass. How could she help falling in love with this man? she wondered desperately. Terrified that her all too expressive face would give too much away, she stuck out her tongue at him and swiftly turned away towards the door.

'It's all right,' she reassured Timmy gruffly as he murmured a little protest. 'I'm just going to fetch our coats.'

What had possessed her to refuse James's proposal out of hand last night? Returning to the lounge, she sat down on the sofa with Timmy and zipped him into his thick padded suit. Did it really matter that much that James didn't love her? Wouldn't it be enough just to be part of his life?

Slipping on her own coat, she carried Timmy across the room. Crouched down, the waxed jacket tautening across the width of his shoulders, James was moulding the snow into shape with his gloved hands. Securing Timmy's hood over his head, Beth slid back the glass door and stepped out onto the balcony, surprised to find the air much warmer than she'd supposed.

Giving the mound of snow one last pat, James rose to his feet and, grinning, raised a quizzical eyebrow.

Her hands tightening around Timmy, Beth grinned back, everything instantly forgotten in the intoxicating pleasure of just looking at James, loving him, being with him. Slowly and thoughtfully she walked round the small, lop-sided and apparently headless snowman, studying it solemnly from every angle.

'Very impressive,' she finally concluded, giving James a look of wide-eyed admiration. 'It really says something to me.'

'Aw, shucks, it's nothing,' James disclaimed modestly, pulling off his damp gloves.

'Yes, I can see that it's nothing,' she agreed, handing Timmy into his waiting arms. Leaning back against the glass door, she watched James drop to his haunches in front of his masterpiece. How could she ever go back to living on her own again?

A little uncertainly Timmy patted the snowman with his small, mittened hands, whereupon it slowly disintegrated into soft powder.

'Hmm.' James straightened up, stamping the snow off his shoes, and surveyed Beth over the top of Timmy's head. 'Maybe I'm a bit out of practice,' he conceded loftily, and his mouth curved in a slow, lazy smile.

Beth's heart constricted as she watched a ray of sunshine caress the thick dark hair. I love you, James Fenner.

Placing Timmy gently back in her arms, James slid back the French doors, standing aside as she stepped by him into the lounge.

After stripping off Timmy's outer clothes, Beth settled him on his mat with his cherished white rabbit and, sitting down beside him, surveyed the room, vividly remembering its pristine, immaculate appearance when she'd first seen it. It most definitely had the lived-in look now, she admitted with a grin as her gaze encompassed the newspapers strewn beside the sofa, Timmy's soft toys scattered on the carpet by his mat and around his rocker.

Her grin widened as she watched James shrug off his jacket and toss it carelessly over the back of a chair. She had a strong suspicion that the flat's previous orderliness had more to do with Mrs Andrews than James's innate tidiness.

'Coffee?' he enquired, and when she nodded her acceptance added casually, with no change of inflection in his voice, 'Will you marry me?'

Beth froze, her eyes jerking to his face. His voice and his expression were as devoid of emotion as if he'd merely been asking her if she required milk in her coffee.

'You didn't think I'd give up that easily, did you?' he said conversationally, sauntering towards the door.

'James!' She jumped to her feet.

He looked at her inquiringly over his shoulder, the

innocence on his face making her want to shake him until his teeth rattled.

'Changed your mind about the coffee? Or about marrying me?'

'And whoever said the age of romance was dead?' Beth ground out through gritted teeth, slumping into a chair.

'Is that what you want?' he said thoughtfully, moving across to the sofa and sitting down. 'You'd like me to sling you across my manly shoulder and whisk you off into the sunset on my white charger?' Folding his hands behind his dark head, he surveyed her tense, slight figure. 'You want me to tell you I can't live without you?'

Yes, I do, you great, insensitive oaf. Jaw clenched, Beth fought back the betraying colour.

'Even though we would both know that it wasn't true?' James asked evenly. 'I can live without you, Beth, but it just so happens that I would prefer to live with you.' He gave a sudden wry smile. 'You infuriate me, exasperate me…'

Oh, great. Beth studied her clenched hands.

'But I'd miss you like hell if you weren't around any more.'

'And that's a good enough reason to marry someone? Because you'd miss them?' Beth looked at him incredulously.

'All marriage is a gamble.' He shrugged. 'But a marriage based on mutual liking, respect and affection probably has as good if not a better chance of succeeding than most.'

Beth swallowed. 'Aren't you missing one tiny little ingredient?'

The dark blue eyes moved over her face. 'If you're asking me if I'm in love with you, the answer is no,' he said quietly.

Beth didn't move, her facial expression frozen into a mask.

'Any more than you're in love with me.' A muscle flickered along his jaw. 'Which has the decided advantage that we will never fall out of love.'

'True.' Beth forced the word out. The numbness was wearing off, pain gnawing into her body. She had never supposed for one moment that he did love her, so why should it hurt so much to hear him confirm it?

She wanted to burst into tears, rush from the room. But she did neither. She just sat there, looking back at him from behind her mask.

'And what happens if you do meet someone and fall in love with them after we're married?' she said, her voice showing no more emotion than if she were raising a point at a board meeting.

His mouth twisted. 'I'm not a teenager, Beth. Credit me with some self-control.'

'You can control who you fall in love with?' Well, he must really be Superman, she thought bitterly.

'I can see an attractive woman without automatically inviting her to share my bed.'

She looked at him squarely. 'I wasn't talking about sex, James. I was talking about love.'

'Which most people use as a palatable euphemism for good old-fashioned lust.'

Beth's eyes locked momentarily with his, the cynicism that had been absent over the past few days very marked in the shadowed blue depths. And it repelled her. This was James Fenner, world-weary, hard-nosed businessman. And for a second she hated him, hated him for replacing the man with the warm, amused eyes, the gentle, humorous face.

'And how does Julia fit into all this?' she asked coolly.

'Julia and I ended our relationship some time ago,' he said quietly. 'But we've remained friends.'

He and Julia no more than friends? Beth looked at him sceptically and saw him frown.

'Do you seriously think that I would have asked you to marry me if I was involved with someone else?' he asked evenly.

As she met the steady gaze Beth flushed slightly. 'No,' she admitted in a small voice, just as she knew instinctively that he would never lie to her or deceive her. If she did marry him and he did meet someone else, she would be the first, not the last, to know. But the pain would still be the same.

She suddenly felt a great well of sympathy for Julia, of whom she'd been so needlessly jealous, and who, she was certain, didn't view James in quite the same platonic light as he did her. She was equally certain that James was innocent of the fact, that he would never knowingly hurt anyone.

She watched him as he rose to his feet and crossed over to the play-mat. Stooping down, he picked up the white rabbit that had fallen out of Timmy's reach and placed it gently back into the tiny hands.

Beth studied the carpet. If only he'd walk across to her now, pull her to her feet, take her in his arms. Show her that he at least wanted her, even if he didn't love her.

But he didn't. He merely returned to the sofa, sat down and surveyed her expectantly. 'Beth?' he prompted.

Slowly she lifted her head. 'Tell me about your marriage,' she said quietly.

CHAPTER NINE

THERE was a brief silence and then, leaning back against the arm-rest, James turned to face her. 'I met Joanne thirteen years ago,' he said without preamble. 'I thought she was the most beautiful woman I had ever seen in my life.' He paused. 'We were married six weeks later.'

Beth studied her hands. Love at first sight. A whirlwind romance. A young, impetuous James, governed by his feelings, not cool logic.

'The marriage lasted two months,' he continued quietly. 'I came home from work one evening and Joanne asked me for a divorce.'

Shocked and incredulous, Beth's eyes flew to James's face. He gave her a grim, humourless smile.

'I was a little surprised myself at the time.' Abruptly he rose to his feet and paced over to the drinks cabinet. He raised an eyebrow at Beth, and when she shook her head poured himself a small measure of whisky then folded his long frame back onto the sofa.

He took a sip from his glass, his eyes focused straight ahead. 'Shortly before I met her, Joanne had been involved with someone else. She wanted him to make some sort of commitment to her, and when he refused she ended the relationship.' The strong, lean fingers tightened imperceptibly around the glass. 'And married me instead. Which proved to be the impetus he needed.'

Beth stared at him uncomprehendingly for a moment, and then she slowly began to understand. 'Once Joanne had married you, her ex-boyfriend decided that he wanted to marry her?' she said in disbelief.

'Apparently he'd turned up a few hours before I arrived home that evening.' Showing no sign of emotion, James tossed the remains of the whisky down the back of his throat. 'Joanne didn't need much persuading. She moved in with him the following day.'

'Joanne married you just to make her boyfriend jealous?' Beth said incredulously, searching the hard, chiselled male features. Didn't he feel bitter? Angry? It was that complete lack of visible emotion, the words left unsaid that somehow made it all the more appalling.

For a second he didn't answer, and then for the first time she saw a flicker of vulnerability in the dark blue eyes. 'No. I don't think she did. Not intentionally,' he finally said quietly, as if it was a conclusion he'd reached after years of indecision. 'She genuinely thought the relationship was over. Probably even believed for a while that she had fallen in love with me.'

'I'm so sorry, James,' Beth muttered. She felt completely useless, knew there was nothing she could do or say to ease his hurt, and for a brief second she hated that faceless woman who had caused his suffering.

'Beth, don't start casting me in the role of tragic hero.'

She flushed. 'I'm not,' she said shortly.

'I've already told you that although my male ego took a bit of a battering I soon realised it was only my pride that was hurt. Nothing more.'

Beth looked back at him evenly. And who are you trying to kid? she thought.

'I wasn't in love and never had been in love with Joanne. Nor she with me. I was twenty-two, still wet behind the ears, naive. I wanted Joanne, but I didn't love her. I was infatuated.' His mouth twisted as if in contempt for his younger self. 'And she married me on the rebound.' He shrugged. 'Even if it hadn't ended quite so abruptly, the marriage wouldn't have had a hope in hell of succeeding.'

'And you think ours would?' Beth said quietly. She very much doubted that James had ever been wet behind the ears. And if he thought the marriage had left him unscarred he was deceiving himself. 'With no messy feelings to get in the way?'

She saw him frown, and rose abruptly to her feet. 'I'm going to see to Timmy's lunch.'

Nodding, he rose to his own feet and went to retrieve the spade from the balcony, closing the French windows behind him.

Beth scooped up Timmy in her arms, and sighed as the telephone in the corner of the room began to ring. It would hardly be for her. She was about to knock on the glass doors to summon James, who was standing motionless by the parapet, when the answering machine clicked on, the brief recorded message followed a few seconds later by a female voice.

'Hi, James…it's Ruthie…'

Beth hurried to the door. She felt uncomfortable listening to a personal call even if it was unintentional.

'Call me back when you get in. I'll be in most of the day. Oh, by the way, I enjoyed meeting Beth at long last. Maybe your taste in women is finally improving…'

Beth paused instinctively and grinned wryly. Thanks, Ruth.

'I suppose you do realise that she's head over heels in love with you, don't you…?'

Beth groaned in disbelief. Oh, Ruth, how could you? She'd have to delete the tape, she thought frantically; she couldn't possibly let James hear that little gem.

But it was too late to do anything. The French doors opened and James stepped back across the threshold.

Hands tightening around Timmy, her face burning with heat, Beth darted into the hall.

She was sitting in the kitchen feeding Timmy when James walked in. It only took one swift glance at his face to know that he'd listened to the tape.

'Yes, it's true,' she said calmly. 'Last mouthful, Tim.' She put the spoon down, wiped the small chin and picked up the bottle, adjusting Timmy's position slightly on her lap. As he started sucking on the bottle, she looked up at the towering figure.

'I love you, James,' she said quietly. She didn't feel awkward or embarrassed, was aware of nothing but a sudden, overwhelming sense of relief at having finally admitted the truth. 'I'm not infatuated with you. And neither do I see you through rose-coloured glasses. I don't think you're perfect. I probably wouldn't love you if you were.' She finally met his eyes and saw the shock in them.

'Oh, hell,' he muttered, and, scraping back a chair,

slumped down onto it. 'I had no idea.' He raked a hand through his dark hair.

'How could you not even suspect it?' Beth felt a surge of anger. 'Ruth guessed straight away!' Her anger faded and she shrugged. 'Anyway, that's why I won't marry you, James,' she continued evenly. 'When or if I ever do get married, I want to be loved in return,' she said simply.

'Beth, I'm sorry,' he murmured.

Her mouth tightened slightly. She didn't want his sympathy. Didn't want him to feel pity for her. 'I want someone who isn't too damn scared to show his feelings.' She looked up at him squarely. 'Love makes you vulnerable, doesn't it, James? And you're too much of a coward to risk ever being hurt again.'

Then, without warning, her composure cracked. She began to tremble, the tears in her throat almost choking her. 'Could you...?' she mumbled.

'Of course,' James said quietly, and, rising to his feet, swiftly and gently took Timmy from her arms. Wordlessly, Beth dived for the door and sped down the hall to the sanctuary of her room.

Throwing herself on her bed, she buried her face in her pillow and sobbed until her chest and throat were raw. Then, rolling over onto her back, she stared bleakly up at the ceiling. She'd get over it. Of course she would. It would stop hurting in time.

'Beth?'

She stiffened as she heard the low voice, and closed her eyes.

'Beth? Are you all right?'

It was no good. She would have to face him again sooner or later. Swinging her legs back onto the carpet, she crossed to the door, dabbing furiously at her eyes before opening it.

For a second, James didn't say anything, his eyes dark with concern as they moved over her tear-stained cheeks. Then he said gruffly, 'Oh, Beth, darling,' and, catching hold of her hands, drew her towards him, pressing her head into his hard shoulder, his arms tightening around her. 'I'm not worth it.'

She was going to cry again, Beth thought desperately. This was ridiculous. James was the last person who should be holding her, comforting her right now.

'I think a hell of a lot of you, Beth,' he muttered near her ear.

Beth eased herself away from him. 'But you don't love me,' she said quietly.

She saw a muscle flicker along his jaw, saw the hesitancy in his eyes, as if he was debating whether to lie to her or not. 'I care about you. I care what happens to you,' he said finally.

Beth shook her head. 'It's not enough,' she said simply. Because one day, despite his conviction to the contrary, some woman would break through that cynicism and James would fall in love. And she didn't want to be standing on the sidelines when it happened.

Her eyes moved slowly over his familiar, beloved features as if committing them to memory for ever, as if it was the last time she would ever see him. She swallowed hard.

'Where's Tim?' she mumbled. Neutral ground. A chance to get herself back in control.

'He's quite happy in his rocker trying to decapitate his rabbit.'

Beth gave a watery smile and cleared her throat. 'I

can't stay here,' she said evenly. 'I'm going back to my flat.'

He frowned. 'Stay until after Christmas, Beth.'

'No.' It would be unbearable now, James skating round her, being kind to her.

'What about Timmy?' he demanded.

'You'll manage,' she said quietly. 'I'm sure the twins will help out.' She didn't want to think about saying goodbye to Timmy. 'In fact you would have managed perfectly well without me all along. There was never any real need for me to come here.' And she wished with all her heart she hadn't. Wished that she had simply gone on adoring James from afar, weaving the occasional little fantasy about him. It had been so safe. 'I don't really know why you ever asked me.'

She saw his eyes darken, something unreadable flicker in the blue shadows.

'No.' He frowned and lapsed into silence, a silence that became increasingly tense. This was how it would be if she did stay—long, awkward silences. It would be unendurable, and she had no intention of prolonging the agony one moment longer.

'I'm going to pack. C-could you call me a taxi, please?' Swiftly she turned back into her room.

'Beth...'

She glanced round.

James shook his head. 'It's not important,' he said vaguely, and, turning on his heel, strode on down the hall.

Mechanically Beth began to collect up her possessions and stow them in her small suitcase. Just concentrate on what you're doing, she told herself. Don't think about tomorrow or Christmas or the future. All the dreary, long days that lie ahead.

Shutting her case, she placed it by the door and walked across to the window. The snow was melting, turning to grey slush in the street below.

She turned round as she heard the knock at the door. 'The taxi's here, Beth.'

Picking up her suitcase, she gave the room one last, cursory glance and, taking a deep breath, opened the door. Silently James took hold of the suitcase and escorted her down the hall.

'Say goodbye to Tim for me,' Beth said lightly.

He nodded.

'Oh, and here's your key,' she added brightly, tugging it out of her jeans pocket and placing it on the hall table. She took hold of her case as he opened the front door, and looked directly up at him for the first time. He'd made no attempt to persuade her to stay for Christmas again, nor had she really expected him to.

'Take care, hmm?' he said softly, and gently touched her face with his hand.

'You t-too,' she mumbled huskily. 'B-better not keep the taxi waiting any longer.' She turned and sped into the waiting lift.

The evening seemed endless. Beth prowled around her small flat, moving from kitchen to bedroom and back into the lounge, flicking on lights and drawing curtains as she went. In a frenetic burst of energy she'd cleaned the flat from top to bottom that afternoon, after making a quick excursion to buy a few basic provisions.

She supposed she ought to have something to eat. Make an omelette, she thought unenthusiastically. James would probably be putting Timmy to bed about now.

Miserably she slumped down in an armchair. And how would he spend the rest of the evening? She suddenly realised that she had no idea how James spent the evenings when he was on his own. But then, she thought, feeling sick, he probably wasn't on his own that often. Not unless it was through choice.

And sometime or other she was going to have to start making plans for the future. Perhaps she wouldn't even apply for another job in London but would move away completely, lessen the risk of ever bumping into James again by chance.

She stared unseeingly at the wall. Surely James wouldn't expect her to work out her month's notice, would he? She'd worry about that later—the office was closed tomorrow anyway, and wouldn't open again till after Christmas. She closed her eyes. Maybe she'd just go to bed. Things always seemed better in the mornings, didn't they?

The next day was even worse. Telling herself that fresh air and exercise were the best remedy, she went out for a walk, pounding the pavements in the vicinity of her flat. It didn't help; everyone she encountered seemed to be part of a couple or a family group. She ended up in a small café on the high street, ordering an endless stream of coffee which she didn't want, knowing that she was simply putting off the inevitable return to her empty flat.

'Beth!'

She collided with David Richardson on the pavement as she left the café. Clutching a multitude of festive parcels, he'd evidently been doing some last-minute shopping.

'Hello.' She forced herself to smile.

He peered down at her as he accompanied her back along the high street in the direction of their respective flats.

'Are you OK? You're not coming down with this flu virus?'

She shook her head. Great—so she looked a mess. She felt a mess, her eyes red and gritty from those weeping jags and lack of sleep.

'I was planning to go over to my parents' later on. They live just outside Windsor.' He paused as they reached her turning. 'But if you fancy going out for a drink tonight I can always go down first thing in the morning,' he said hopefully.

For a moment she was tempted. Anything would be better than spending another solitary evening. But it wouldn't be fair to use him like that. 'I'm sorry, David, but I can't make it tonight.'

He smiled. 'Maybe after Christmas?'

She smiled noncommittally. She did like David. Perhaps once she had James out of her system…

'Happy Christmas.' He stooped and kissed her lightly on the cheek as they parted.

'Happy Christmas, David.' Turning away, she began to walk slowly down her street.

And how long was it going to take her to get James out of her system? She fished out her front-door keys from her coat pocket and entered the communal hall. A few months? Years? She squared her small chin and took a deep breath. Of course she'd get over him in time. She was not going to spend the rest of her life wanting a man who didn't love her, and feeling this wretched. Her hands clenched into fists. She wasn't!

Her resolve evaporated the second she walked into her silent, empty flat. What was he doing now? she wondered despondently. Just over twenty-four hours and she ached so much to see him again, hear his voice, the pain twisting inside her like a knife. Had he thought about her? Missed her even the teeniest bit?

Stop it, Beth. Stop it! And then suddenly she was too drained, too tired to think or care about anything any more. Mechanically she went into the kitchen to make herself a sandwich, forced herself to eat it and then, returning to the lounge, curled up on the settee. Her eyes closed as exhaustion finally claimed her.

Beth stretched out a hand to switch off the insistent alarm clock, and tumbled off the settee. Disorientated, she scrambled to her feet, and blinked at her surroundings. Why wasn't she in bed? What time was it? That was the telephone...

She padded into her bedroom and picked up the extension on her bedside table.

'Beth?' the familiar, deep voice grunted in her ear.

'Do you know...?' she began automatically, her brain still fuddled with sleep.

'Yes. It's thirteen minutes past four,' James growled. 'Timmy's missing you,' he added abruptly.

'At this time in the morning?' Beth growled back, and put the phone down, sinking weakly onto the edge of the bed. The telephone rang again almost immediately.

'I miss you,' grunted the disembodied voice.

Beth swallowed. 'It's not enough.' She cut the line and lay back on her pillow. One, two, three. She picked up the receiver again.

'I love you, Beth Sinclair,' James thundered. 'I need you. I want you. Dammit, I love you!'

Tears welling in her eyes, Beth expelled a long, shuddering breath. Thank God.

'Beth? Are you still there?'

'Mmm. Sorry, but I didn't quite catch that. What did you say just then?' Misty-eyed, Beth grinned inanely at the phone.

'You heard me,' James growled. 'The taxi'll be there in ten minutes.'

Talk about assumptions! 'James Fenner, if you think you have only to crook your little finger and I'll come running...'

'Eight minutes.' The phone went dead.

'You're absolutely right,' Beth informed the bedside table with an idiotic smile.

'Will you marry me, Beth Sinclair?'

Gently, Beth stretched up a hand and caressed the strong, assured face only inches away from hers.

'Why do you want to marry me?' she asked with wide, innocent eyes. Now this was more like it. Curled up beside James on his sofa, the room illuminated by the coloured lights on the Christmas tree.

The straight mouth quirked. 'Because I love you.' His arms tightening around her, James drew her effortlessly onto his lap.

'I know,' she murmured, her eyes glowing with happiness as they locked with his. How could she doubt it for a moment when he looked at her like that? 'And yes, please.'

'I've been such a damn fool,' James said huskily. 'I've been falling in love with you for months, but I refused to accept it, wouldn't admit what I was feeling. I was so terrified...'

'Of being hurt again,' Beth said gently.

'No.' He shook his head. 'I've already told you I was never in love with Joanne,' he said softly. 'And that's what terrified me—making the same mistake again. I didn't trust my own feelings any more.' He paused. 'I knew I was attracted to you, was from the moment you first walked into my office.'

Beth looked at him in astonishment. 'You were?' She batted her eyelashes at him. 'All that time you were mad with desire for me and I had absolutely no idea.'

'I'm not in the habit of making passes at my secretary,' he said primly.

'I should think not,' she informed him reprovingly. 'Though you could have made an exception for once,' she added with a grin.

'Hussy.' He gave her a long, lingering kiss.

Beth sighed blissfully as he lifted his head, and slid her fingers through his rich, dark hair, stroking it back from his forehead, remembering how many times she had ached to do just that. 'I love you so much,' she whispered, nuzzling his throat.

James hugged her so hard that she thought he would squeeze the breath from her body. 'I still can't believe what an idiot I've been, how much time I've wasted,' he said wryly, easing his hold. 'I started missing you at weekends, started deliberately creating work so that I could ask you to come into the office on Saturdays, stay late in the evenings.'

'James Fenner, of all the devious...'

'And even then I still refused to face the truth,' he continued ruefully, and then grinned. 'And I used my own nephew to coerce you into moving in with me!'

'Now that is really deplorable,' Beth admonished him severely.

'I could have employed a nanny until either the twins or Anna were free,' he admitted, and dropped his head back against the sofa. 'Served me right, because having you around proved to be an exquisite form of torture.' He groaned. 'Knowing you were lying just a few feet away from me every night when I wanted you in my bed.' His mouth sought hers with fierce urgency.

Her eyes closing, Beth's arms locked around his neck, feeling him shudder against her as she kissed him back.

'Beth...' He muttered her name raggedly as he pushed her back on the sofa, stretching out beside her. His mouth covering hers again, his hands swept possessively down the length of her body, tightened around her hips, pulling her into him. Then, with a groan, he let his hands fall abruptly to his sides.

'Timmy.' Swinging his long legs onto the carpet, he stood up.

Beth peered at her watch as she too heard the tiny, waking cry. 'It's seven o'clock!' She registered the time with disbelief. 'Morning.'

'Christmas Day,' James said softly, and, holding

out a hand, pulled her to her feet. 'Happy Christmas, Beth.' Reaching into the pocket of his jeans, he pulled out a small jeweller's box.

Her hands trembling, Beth opened it slowly. 'Oh, James, it's b-beautiful,' she mumbled, gazing down at the exquisite diamond ring.

'Tim and I chose it yesterday,' he said casually.

Beth's eyes blurred as he carefully took the ring from the box and slipped it on the third finger of her left hand. 'Timmy has excellent taste.' She was laughing through her tears. 'You bought it yesterday? You were very sure of yourself, James Fenner.'

'No. Just sure of my feelings,' he said softly.

'Why did you wait until four o'clock this morning to tell me, then?'

For a moment she thought he wasn't going to answer, and then he murmured vaguely, 'Actually Tim and I drove over to your flat in the afternoon...'

'You did? But...'

'I saw you walking along the street with David Richardson,' he confessed. 'And I was so damn jealous I drove straight home.'

'Oh, James.' Beth laughed softly, her eyes brimming with love. 'David and I have never been anything more than friends. There's never been anyone else but you, and never will be.'

For a second he stood motionless, didn't touch her, didn't say anything, but the expression in his eyes made her feel giddy.

Then slowly he drew her into his arms, looking down with surprise as he felt her stiffen.

'Beth?'

'I haven't bought you a present,' she wailed, her eyes darting to the packages under the tree.

'No socks?' James murmured, crestfallen.

'No aftershave,' Beth said sadly as his hold on her tightened.

'I've everything I want for Christmas and the rest of my life right here,' he said huskily.

'Have you?' she muttered unsteadily, her eyes fixed on the firm mouth just above hers.

'Timmy,' they both reminded the other in unison, and, grinning, headed for the door.

'I'll get his bottle.' James turned into the kitchen.

'I'll change him.' Beth sped on down the hall. Team work, she mused, and smiled ecstatically.

'Guess what, Tim? I'm going to marry your uncle James!' She picked him up and hugged him. 'You're the first person I've told,' she added earnestly.

Her small confidant surveyed her solemnly for one long moment, and then beamed.

Beth frowned. Had she imagined that look of utter relief in those huge, innocent blue eyes?

EPILOGUE

'SHALL I push it now for a bit, Timmy?' Beth murmured peacefully.

'No. Me do it.' His face flushed with exertion, Timmy determinedly weaved an erratic, unsteady path across the grass with his pushchair.

Beth sauntered by his side, keeping a vigilant eye out for potential casualties. Hampstead Heath was busy this Sunday afternoon with walkers, joggers, picnickers—all taking advantage of the warm June sunshine.

Abandoning his pushchair, Timmy squatted down on his small haunches, carefully picked a daisy and handed it gravely to Beth.

'Thank you, darling.'

'Kiss.'

Obediently Beth stooped down and kissed the velvety cheek.

'Shall we catch up with Uncle James?' Shielding her eyes against the sun, Beth grinned as she gazed at the lean, stationary figure a few yards ahead of them. An expression of unconvincing nonchalance on his face, James was chatting to three elderly women who were cooing into the large pram in front of him.

'They asked me which was which, and I was damned if I could remember,' he muttered with a frown as Beth joined him.

Beth sighed. 'Now this is the last time I'll go over

it with you, so pay attention,' she said severely. 'The one with the dark hair and pink, screwed-up little face is your son.'

James nodded attentively.

'And the one with the dark hair and pink, screwed-up little face is your daughter.'

'Right.' James looked thoughtful.

Beth grinned. And the one with the dark hair and dazzling blue eyes is my husband, she added silently.

Timmy peeped into the pram. 'Two babies,' he said with satisfaction, as if fearing that his uncle might have mislaid one of his tiny cousins during the afternoon.

'Twins. Like Aunt Ruth and Aunt Becky.' Beth smiled down at him and then glanced at her watch. 'Caroline's picking Tim up at four.'

'Start heading for home?' James raised an eyebrow.

She nodded. Home for the last year had been a spacious house with a large garden overlooking the heath.

'Kiss.' Timmy beamed up at her.

Beth stooped down and obliged.

'Kiss.' James beamed down at her.

Beth stretched up and obliged.

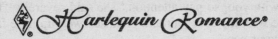

Take 4 bestselling love stories FREE

Plus get a FREE surprise gift!

Coming in August 1997!

THE BETTY NEELS RUBY COLLECTION

August 1997—Stars Through the Mist
September 1997—The Doubtful Marriage
October 1997—The End of the Rainbow
November 1997—Three for a Wedding
December 1997—Roses for Christmas
January 1998—The Hasty Marriage

COLLECTOR'S EDITION

This August start assembling the
Betty Neels Ruby Collection. Six of the
most requested and best-loved titles have
been especially chosen for this collection.
From August 1997 until January 1998,
one title per month will be available to avid
fans. Spot the collection by the lush ruby red
cover with the gold Collector's Edition banner
and your favorite author's name—Betty Neels!

Available in August at your favorite retail outlet.

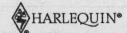

HARLEQUIN®

Look us up on-line at: http://www.romance.net   BNRUBY

Free Gift Offer

With a Free Gift proof-of-purchase
from any Harlequin® book, you can receive
a beautiful cubic zirconia pendant.

This stunning marquise-shaped stone is a genuine cubic
zirconia—accented by an 18" gold tone necklace.
(Approximate retail value $19.95)

Send for yours today...
compliments of ⬦HARLEQUIN®

To receive your free gift, a cubic zirconia pendant, send us one original proof-of-purchase, photocopies not accepted, from the back of any Harlequin Romance®, Harlequin Presents®, Harlequin Temptation®, Harlequin Superromance®, Harlequin Intrigue®, Harlequin American Romance®, or Harlequin Historicals® title available at your favorite retail outlet, together with the Free Gift Certificate, plus a check or money order for $1.65 U.S./$2.15 CAN. (do not send cash) to cover postage and handling, payable to Harlequin Free Gift Offer. We will send you the specified gift. Allow 6 to 8 weeks for delivery. Offer good until December 31, 1997, or while quantities last. Offer valid in the U.S. and Canada only.

Free Gift Certificate

Name: _____

Address: _____

City: _____ State/Province: _____ Zip/Postal Code: _____

Mail this certificate, one proof-of-purchase and a check or money order for postage and handling to: HARLEQUIN FREE GIFT OFFER 1997. In the U.S.: 3010 Walden Avenue, P.O. Box 9071, Buffalo NY 14269-9057. In Canada: P.O. Box 604, Fort Erie, Ontario L2Z 5X3.

FREE GIFT OFFER   084-KEZ
ONE PROOF-OF-PURCHASE
To collect your fabulous FREE GIFT, a cubic zirconia pendant, you must include this
original proof-of-purchase for each gift with the properly completed Free Gift Certificate.

084-KEZR

WELCOME TO *Love Inspired* ™

A brand-new series of contemporary inspirational love stories.

Join men and women as they learn valuable lessons about facing the challenges of today's world and about life, love and faith.

Look for:

Promises
by Roger Elwood

A Will and a Wedding
by Lois Richer

An Old-Fashioned Love
by Arlene James

Available in retail outlets
in October 1997.

LIFT YOUR SPIRITS AND GLADDEN YOUR HEART with *Love Inspired* ™!

Steeple
Hill™

LI1197